A TASTE OF
TERRORISM

By
D. J. McAllister

ISBN: 978-0-578-40116-4

Design: Dedicated Book Services, www.http://dedicatedbooks.com/

DEDICATION

This book is dedicated to all the Military members,
Veterans, First Responders and Emergency Personnel
who save our lives and protect the American People
on a daily basis.

Many thanks to Betty, who without her,
these books would not have been completed.

Please post a photo of this cover on Facebook,
or other media so your friends and their friends
will know where to buy this book.

AMAZON.COM / Books / djmcallister

Contents

A Taste of Terrorism

Chapter 1

Springs Stained Glass

We have been on the road for a few weeks and Lopez and I voted that we should give everyone a few days off in a row as a bonus. Everyone gets a three day weekend even if it's in the middle of the week. I got Wednesday through Friday of the next week.

Wednesday turned out to be a nice day and I was sitting in the back yard on my favorite lawn chair having some iced tea and not thinking about anything. But Denise had to muddy up the water.

She came and sat down next to me.

"DJ, could I talk to you about something?" She said.

"Uh, huh."

Sometimes I answer when I shouldn't and I always get in trouble for it.

"Do you know what I would really like?" She said.

Now how would I know that? But I always answer her, no matter how silly the question is. But this time she continued without taking a breath to let me speak.

"You enjoy sitting out here and I enjoy it too. When we have friends over, like Lopez and when Ted and Eve come, we always come out here." She said.

That was only the preamble to her answer. Now comes the meat.

"I wish we could have a screenroom here on the back of the house. It could open out on to a nice big patio where we could have twenty or thirty chairs, couches and gliders for people to sit on." She said.

I would bet there is more to come. Take a deep breath.

"I bet it wouldn't cost very much. We built those rooms on the house in Wichita for only a few thousand." She said.

That was many years ago and she hasn't kept up with the pricing of what she is talking about.

"The room could go from that corner of the house to that corner next to the garage and we would have all this space for a nice big patio for everyone." She said.

You'll notice that I haven't had a chance to speak since she sat down.

"I don't know who we could get to do the work, but since you know everyone in town, maybe you could. But even better, maybe you could do it all yourself. You know all about construction by now, don't you?"

That was a long dissertation, maybe she will take a breath now. Now's my chance.

"Don't you think that a project like this would take more than one unprofessional person to do, and that they would be able to finish, or even start?"

Her idea sounds good, but her followup is all wrong.

"Tell you what, I will give you some names of contractors and builders, and you get some bids. But before you do that, you need a design on paper.

Something for them to look at that shows sizes and placement of the main items."

That should keep her busy for a while.

Years ago, when I started going to the Colorado Springs Christian Church, I found that I was enjoying the pastors sermons and that he taught everything out of the book. If it wasn't in the book, then he usually made no mention of it.

One day the pastor told us about some classes in stained glass building that were being offered by a stained glass company in town. Since I had the opportunity to take the classes then and learn something new, I jumped at the chance.

When we think window, we think wood frame, a piece of glass, stick it in the hole in the wall and screw it in, done. It's not the same with those colored windows.

What I found out was that this is not the easiest thing to do. The classes were eight weeks long two days a week, and you got to make a window or a sun-catcher as you went.

I dutifully went to the shop where the classes were being held and worked very hard to understand the directions and put everything I was told into actual practice. But, alas, I didn't have the talent for this artistic work.

During the time I wasted with this, I met a really nice guy named Earl Cohen. He is about my age and knows the glass business very well. It is his business that is providing the classes. He said he learned it in high school, and has been doing it since then.　He showed me pictures of some of his work, I believe he is a true genius in this field.

One Sunday after the classes were finished, we were standing around after a lunch in the church basement when he signaled me that he wanted to talk.

"Hi DJ. Could I get you to help me once in a while with the glass if I needed it?" He said.

"Sure, be glad to, but I'm no good at it as you saw in those classes. What kind of help would you need?"

"Sometimes the windows are too large and heavy for me to lift them.　And then I have to remove nails and screws or put them in after I'm done." He said.

"By the way, what kind of work do you do?" He asked.

"Oh, I'm in law enforcement." I tried to say it as quietly as possible so it wouldn't be a big thing.

"What do you do?"

"Oh, I'm the assistant pastor here." He said.

Oh boy, I didn't know that.

Since it's very hard to do the necessary work on the windows, he needed someone to be the chauffeur, carrier, lifter, holder, gopher, and janitor for him.　I love to kid him about this. I know it's really hard to get anything done when you must get down off of a ladder and find a tool that you forgot you would need.

So now I work with him about once a month.　I enjoy it so much that I sometimes take Denise with Earl and I for the day.

I am sure that he doesn't know what I do for a living. He probably wouldn't have asked me to help him if he did.

I found out that he was right about the heavy windows. The first one I helped him with weighed about forty pounds. I found out over time that as your age number goes up, so does the weight number of the glass go up.

After the eight weeks, I finished the classes and made something for my wife. She loves cardinals, so I did my best, but it's definitely not up to the standard. Earl picked up my Cardinal and made it look like a bird, not a red blotch on a tree.

I can put the windows in and take them out, but I'll leave the designing and building to a more artistic person like Earl.

It turned out that Earl is a sheer genius in this area, and he normally only does churches, because no one else will, but I have helped him at someone's house a time or two. Maybe he is the only one in town that does this kind of thing.

He does all the measuring, drawing, cutting, soldering, welding and wood work necessary to finish the window. All I do is help with the lifting and carrying.

Last year a big hail storm came through and totally destroyed the windows in the big chapel at the university. It seems like we were working on it ever since. There are six windows on each side of the building, each window has a pair of windows side by side and a small one under them in the same frame. The way I count that is thirty windows.

After the big hail storm we had here, he convinced the school to install lexan on the outside of the windows so the hail wouldn't break the glass. They had put Plexiglas outside before, to cover and protect the windows, but the hail destroyed it. We always remove the cheap Plexiglas now, it's broken most of the time anyway.

Lexan must be made out of lead. It is amazingly heavy for something so thin and transparent. One thing about it is this, it will stop hail, and lead.

Earl will build one window while I am out of town and I will always call him when I get back after I stop by to see Norm and see how the Foundation is doing. Sometime during the next few days we would install the finished window and remove the next one. Seems like a good plan.

I have always enjoyed this work, because I am doing something for someone else that isn't in the criminal element.

The windows in the University Chapel are eight feet tall and twenty inches wide and each complete window has two of these side by side mounted above a louver type window that is supposed to swing open like a jalousie. This little window is eighteen inches high and the full width of the two tall ones.

Earl and I can usually read each others minds, and we know what the other is doing and what they will do next.

We were installing one of the tall window panels that he had just finished the week before.

These things are very heavy and hard to handle. Besides that they are all mounted above the floor at the best height to catch the most light from the sun. We have a rolling scaffold that we use to move around the room and give us the height we need.

I had the panel raised up onto the sill and he was on a ladder holding the top of the panel, ready to put it in place. There is only eighteen inches left to go. Suddenly the panel began to swing toward my back and it fell down over my head and wrapped around my back. All this only took a few seconds.

"Earl! I have the panel down here."

"Oh! That's where it went." He said. "I'll be right down!"

Nothing seems to bother him, but he came down in a flash.

I couldn't help but laugh at his comment. He is always so positive about everything.

It's a good thing I wear an old baseball cap when I do this. There were pieces of colored glass all around us on the scaffold and the floor.

He helped me get the broken panel off of me and onto the scaffold.

"I only let go of it for a second and it decided to fly away." He said. "Let's get this all cleaned up. We're not going to be any good for the rest of the day." After a short pause, he said. "Let's go get a hamburger or something."

It took us another hour to get the glass picked up out of the carpet and off of the scaffold. We collected all the tools and moved the scaffold to a place where it wouldn't be as noticeable. Then we headed for his big green Chevy van and drove away.

I know that he is joking to keep from crying. These panels have a huge number of pieces of glass in them. And they are all different colors and shapes. The time alone it took to build this one panel must have been huge. Now he has to start from scratch and finish it again.

"I guess I have my work broken out for me this time." He said.

Fortunately, we finished the University Chapel some time ago and now we only see it from the outside as we drive by.

He wanted to pay me for the work I did for him, but I explained about the Foundation and I gave him money instead. I don't think he believed me about the Foundation, so I took him to meet Norm and see some of the miracles that he performs at his shop.

"Look at these cars!" He said. "Wow! That's a '62 Chevy!" Then he walked near a '51 Ford. "I had one of these!" He said and pointed at it. He walked around the shop and looked at everything.

"He gets excited doesn't he?" Norm said.

"Yeah. Only about cars though. I've known him for a little while and I notice that he really likes the old cars. We should build him one."

"Is this what you were talking about when you said the Foundation?" Earl said.

"Yeah. We give away about one or two cars a week. But the people have to qualify for one. They only go to people who can't afford them." Norm said.

"Too bad you can't have stained glass in a car. I would really enjoy, no, laugh a lot with a stained glass window in a car." Earl said.

Chapter 2

Indianapolis

Last year, we spent most of our time hunting for terrorists. A few of the sweeps through the schools in the cities in the Midwest uncovered terrorists posing as teachers and professors. I really don't like terrorists, but the combination of teachers and terrorists makes me mad.

We were fed some information on the whereabouts of a group of teachers and professors who were teaching the students to hate America and all the people who live here. Lieutenant Lopez, the commander of the Cyber Crimes Division, called a meeting and gave out all the info. Then he asked for volunteers to go round up this group.

"There you have it! I have told you everything about this project that I have. I would like a couple of volunteers to help me with picking these people up and housing them here in our cross-bar hotel until the feds can take them away." He said.

Every person in the room held up their hand. That's the kind of response that I just love to see.

We arrested eight of the crooks and sent five of them to jail in our favorite little town in Kansas. We all felt good about what we had achieved and forgot all about the whole operation. Of the other three, one of them had escaped from jail in Missouri and stole a car and got away. All we knew was that he traveled east. I put the word out on him with pictures and prints and he was picked up a few months later in Indiana.

"Boy, it's good to sit back and take it easy once in a while."

"Yeah! We've been running for a few months now." Lopez said.

Lieutenant Lopez and I had been sitting in his office drinking coffee and enjoying a slow time in the crime business for the past few days when a Process Server walked into his office and handed us both one of those little pieces of paper with our names on them. What a way to end a nice restful day at noon. And we haven't even had lunch yet. I guess there's no rest for the weary.

Neither Lopez nor I like leaving home to go on the road for anybody, but when a subpoena appears in your hand, you go. No questions. All I did was arrest him. What do they need me for? Especially in Indianapolis. Oh well, here we go for a drive across the country to put some scum in jail, I hope.

Lopez and I both agreed to drive rather than fly this time so we could stop on the way back and see Mike and the rest of them in Kansas City.

There's always a lot of prep work we must complete before a road trip. I always need to check my disguises. This time was no different.

In addition, we need a good map, the address of the courthouse, and some names of the people who demand our presence and attention at this up-coming trial.

Indianapolis is certainly the largest city in the state with at least a million residents. I wouldn't even guess how many square miles it covers. We got lucky and I-70 runs right through the middle of it. Now we have the address of the courthouse, so that should be easy to find. I hope.

I always get my darling wife, Denise, a souvenir from every city or town we visit. I hope one of the cops might be able to tell me where to find something special for her.

We spent several days in Indianapolis where they caught this creep. We did enjoy sampling the food, listening to lawyers talk, not so much, and just having so much fun. We couldn't wait to get out of there. We both loved the town, but all the arguing and wrangling that we witnessed inside that big building, I could have done without. And it just went on and on and on. But it is an integral part of our justice system, so we put up with it.

One good thing that we witnessed and enjoyed to the full was this. The escaped terrorist was sentenced to spend what was left of his miserable life in a little town just north of Kansas City called Leavenworth. I'm sure he will love it there.

After a week of trial, witnesses, lawyers, and court-room antics, Lopez and I were ready to be on our way out of Indianapolis after our court appearance we had been subpoenaed for. I sat around all day and was not called upon to say a word. Lopez and I were glad when it was over. We all got lucky and put another terrorist in, I hope under, the jail.

One of the local PD guys brought me a picture with the words 'Indiana State Bird' on it. It's a cardinal. The cardinal is a popular state bird. I know I got one from Missouri for my darling wife, Denise, some years ago. She'll love this.

"Thanks a lot Sam. I would have missed this. I know she'll love this."

I gave him the money to pay for it and we were on our way.

Now it's finally time to go home. As we were driving out of town looking for I-70 I was filling the magazine in my favorite little nine millimeter friend, James Bond, when Lopez said. "Quick! Look there!" And pointed to a man. He had spotted a man walking on the sidewalk and we both recognized him. This was the latest terrorist professor that we had been hunting for a month or more.

Lopez swerved to stop him and I jumped out of the car and showed him James Bond and he stopped and raised his hands. I slipped the bracelets on him and put him in the back seat behind Lopez with me beside him. I've been told that I like to be close to my work.

We sat and I talked to him for a short while. But this time he surprised me. I quickly grabbed my

recorder and turned it on. And as with all the terrorist professors, he told us how smart he was and how
stupid all the Americans were. I have heard their
speech so many times, I could probably quote it from
memory.

"We have taken over your education system in this
country. We have been teaching all your children to
hate you and your corrupt hateful country for many
years now. There is nothing you can do about it.
Ha, ha, ha." The Professor said.

"Wait a minute! What do you mean?"

"We have established the 'EL Party'. That stands
for the 'Everybody Loves' party. We like the name,
it suits you. We were surprised at how many of your
so called 'loyal' Americans have joined us in our plan
to take over and destroy this country. We have teachers, bankers, journalists, politicians and influential
people in all walks of life helping us here." He said.

"You stupid Americans think you understand terrorism and what it is about. You don't understand
anything! You have only had a taste of terrorism!
We will be feeding you much more! There is no way
you can stop us now!", he said. He began to chuckle
about what he had said. He is getting on my nerves.

Lopez has been listening to him and driving very
slowly with a scowl on his face.

It was only a few blocks later that we saw a young
woman looking so forlorn. She was standing in the
middle of a bridge and looking down over the rail.
It looked like she was thinking about jumping off.

I could see that Lopez just had to stop and see what we could do for her. We still haven't driven out of town as yet. Lopez got out of the car to help her. For a cop, Lopez is a real softie. Once he got her to talking, and not thinking about jumping, everything slowed down to normal.

I helped her into the back seat and put the seat belt on. I made sure she was comfortable and Lopez took off.   We began to question her and I made sure my recorder was still running.

She explained to us what she was doing in town and where she wanted to go. She had lost her job because she couldn't put up with the nasty actions of her boss and she was moving on to find a job and a place to stay.

She rejected the advances of her boss and since she wouldn't give in, he fired her. I found out from her where she worked and what her bosses name was. I immediately called one of our undercover partners in the city and gave him all the details I had.

She said that she had reported it to a supervisor up the line in the company, but they did not believe her. More needs to be done here. Bill said that he would scrub the dirt out of that company. I believe him.

"Where were you going and do you have any family or friends to stay with?" I asked her.

"My family lives on the east coast, and it is too far to go for them to come and get me. I don't have any friends anymore. I'm just moving away to start a new life, but I don't know where to go." She said.

I had to move to the front seat to let her in the car, so I made sure that the professor was handcuffed to the locked door but once we got onto the freeway and up to speed, he tried to assault her.

I'm always amazed at the stupidity of criminals. This guy is handcuffed and locked to the door, and yet he makes a group of ridiculous motions to try to get to the girl, with Lopez driving and me holding a gun pointed at him. I suppose he thought we would stop and let him out of the car if he caused trouble.

But, as Bugs Bunny used to say. "He don't know me, do he?"

The professor had ripped her shirt open with his teeth and was trying to get her undressed and embarrassed. He wrestled around like a wild man. She smacked him a couple times, but that seemed like it emboldened him and he tried harder.

He had just told me that there was no way to stop him. I decided to show him one way that I knew that always worked for me. I showed him James Bond and JB spoke to him. JB usually stops every discussion he is involved in.

"Physstt!"

I put one in his chest and he immediately stopped what he was doing. That's one way that always works.

She was shocked and said. "Who are you guys and who was he?"

I grabbed Lopez's badge and showed it to her and said, "We were taking him to jail. He is a terrorist. But now I have to call Mike."

I didn't need to show her my badge. It might have scared her. She spent some time getting herself put back together both physically and emotionally, and I called Mike.

"Hey Mike, its One Shot. Lopez and I have a young woman who is looking for a job and a place to stay. Do you have anything there that she can do?"

"What can she do?" Mike asked.

"Well she just fought off a terrorist professor in our back seat. I had to have James Bond speak to him, so the discussion is over. By the way we will need a place to deposit our passenger."

"I think I can accommodate you on all your requests. Bring it on. I'll see you at the bar. Where are you?" Mike said.

"We're about halfway to St. Louis from Indianapolis. We're stopped in Effingham for gas. It'll be a few more hours. See you in about four hundred miles."

After the gas stop, I took the wheel and we were off and running at seventy five on the cruise control. It was still light at six when I started. We made Columbia by nine thirty and Lopez took his turn. We made KC by a quarter to eleven and I was done in. It's been a long few days.

"It would help if I knew your name and some other details"

"My name is Amber O'Reilly." She went on to fill in the blanks for me.

I asked her every question I could think of so that I could get her words on the recorder I carry. We talked about everything. I'll give it to Mike and they can play it.

Around Independence I offered to drive, but Lopez is stubborn, and he kept on going. I could tell he was tired too. We decided to talk and try to keep each other awake and alert.

Lopez stayed with it and took us through town to Platte City. It could have been a good hours drive just to get through town but we got lucky. There was not much traffic at the time and Lopez was in a hurry. It's a good thing that the car didn't have red lights and siren, because he would have had them on too.

Finally we stopped at Mike's Family Restaurant at midnight. I still have a key, but there was one light on and the door was unlocked.

Sally was there and she took care of Amber. Sally had some food ready for us all and she showed Amber to a room upstairs where she could sleep.

Mike and I took the professor to the morgue and left him there. Glad to get rid of him. When we got back to the bar Lopez was asleep in one of the booths, and Sally was cleaning up.

Mike always needs to know everything at the instant it happens. Here he comes with questions. I can see it in his eyes.

"OK! Who is she?" Mike asked.

"Her name is Amber O'Reilly."

"Amber O'Reilly. O'Reilly! Oh really?" Mike said.

"Yeah! And don't gimme any of your funny talk. That's Irish!"

"I know what Irish is! I'm Irish, too. My name's McCoy, remember McAllister?" Mike said.

"My name's McCoy too, and I have a number in my name. One Shot. That means I'm special." I had to laugh at that. I don't usually get one over on Mike.

"OK. You're right, we have to help her, because it's the right thing to do." He said.

Chapter 3

Woman In Distress

In the morning, I bounced out of bed, did my shave, shower and everything routine and put on some of Mike's best clothes and went down to the bar for breakfast. Nice that they are the right size. I especially liked the jacket. I don't usually get dressed up in a suit and tie, but it was there begging me to wear it.

Sally was there with a pitcher of coffee and a menu before I reached the booth.

"Hi, Mike! Oh! It's you! Nice jacket. Looks like one I've seen before." She said and chuckled a little.

"Hi Sal. I would love two eggs, hash browns, toast and coffee. Thanks."

She smiled a canned waitress smile, and walked toward the kitchen.

They were all there before the eggs came. Mike and Lieutenants Brown and Lopez were sitting in the booth with me, looking like I should be paying attention to each one of them. They all had coffee with them. I continued with my eggs and listened to each of them as much as I could as they talked about things I didn't know about and didn't want to talk about until I stopped chewing.

"We need a plan!" Brown said. "I'll get on the background and clearance of the girl right now.

Lopez and Mike questioned her and took all the information they could from her."

They all seemed to be talking at the same time. And I wasn't listening to any of it.

"We played the tape DJ made, she sounds OK so far. Maybe she could use the phone and that would free us up to chase the crooks." Mike said.

"We could have her call all the guys in the area and ask them to come and help us here till we got things cleaned up." Lopez said. "I'll start the background check and clearance. Can she stay here with Sally and get started?"

"Sure." Mike said.

Later in the morning, while we tried to resolve all the questions and problems we had acquired, Lopez and I went driving through KC to think and do a little brainstorming.

"You think we can use her?" Lopez asked.

"Sure, why not"

"I'll see what I can find out on her. Shouldn't be too hard." Lopez said. "We need to find out what her job was and her education." He said.

"OK. I'll try Ted for his help too."

We had been driving for almost an hour and we were not going anywhere in particular when we saw a woman holding the body of another older woman lying on the sidewalk.

Lopez stopped and I slowly and silently approached the two. There was a man standing next to them and he was smiling a huge smile and holding a gun in his hand.

She turned and asked him if he had shot the woman.

He smiled again and said, "Yes!", proudly, and waved the gun around as if it were a trophy. He acted and moved like it was his right to shoot this woman.

She reached into her purse and pulled out a little chrome plated snub nosed thirty two caliber revolver and shot him once in the stomach. I know that had to hurt.

"BANG".

His huge smile faded into a look of surprise and he staggered slightly and dropped the pistol on the sidewalk.

"But she deserved it!" He said as loudly as he could between the huffing and puffing.

She shot him a second time in a place slightly higher on his body. More pain and he screamed a little after this one.

"BANG".

"Your mother was a whore!" He said in a weaker voice than before. He was trying to justify his shooting.

"BANG".

She shot him the third time in the solar plexus and it was lights out for him. He fell down on the sidewalk almost right in front of her.

"Well, I guess you won't be killing anyone else's mother now." She said. And calmly put the pistol back in her purse and hugged her mother again and began to cry.

I leaned over her and quietly said, "Give me the gun." She handed me the purse and I pocketed it and said, "I'll take care of this one." I motioned to the man and his gun. I carefully put his gun in a bag to give to Lopez.

I called to the car. "Hey Lopez, you better take a look at this."

I put cuffs on him and Lopez and I loaded him into the trunk. This is getting to be a habit.

"Why the cuffs?" Lopez asked.

"Just for looks."

He listened as I explained what I had just seen and we loaded the body into the trunk and put the woman and her mother in the back seat. I gave him directions to the nearest PD and Lopez hotfooted it into the station and we had a few officers help with the problem in the trunk. I haven't any idea what the outcome of this will be, but I will help the woman as much as I can.

"I think that man was another of those crazy terrorists, but I'm not sure." I told the Desk Sergeant.

Our trip from Indiana netted us two women that we don't know and don't know what to do with.

Both Lieutenants were working feverishly to figure out a plan for them. I'm stuck until we learn something about them.

Lieutenant Brown gave us a rundown on the girl and the two other people. The girl hugging her mother on the street is an immigrant from Egypt. The man who did the shooting was an assassin sent by her father to kill both her and her mother.

"What's her name?

"Oh, I forgot. It's here somewhere. Here it is. Nema Jabbar, she's Egytian." He said.

The girl was a legal immigrant of about fifteen years ago. Her mother came here a few years later and they have been living together. Her mother had applied for citizenship two years later.

We also found out that her immigrant mother was a political activist against the radical rebels in her country. It looks like that was the reason that they sent the assassin to eliminate her. I told the PD that it was a justifiable shooting on her part.

We checked all her papers and cleared her of illegal entry. But now the mother and the assassin are dead and the daughter has fallen into depression from the killing of her mother.

I'm going to send all the information on this little event to a friend of mine in Egypt. I hope he can clear up all the details that are left.

Amber is a really different one. She had a good job as a high school teacher. But because she had worked with a PD in the east near her home, she had those instincts. She did some investigating and found out that her boss was on the side of the terrorists and their friends. He is being held for questioning. I'll volunteer Amber to make up some questions for him.

Fortunately she made a call to the USSS and reported him. How he found out about that I don't know, but we have a leak and we better plug it fast.

We've spent too much time in Kansas City now and it's time to get back on the road again. See there, I'm a song writer too.

The trip from Kansas City to Colorado Springs is about seven hundred miles. And it gets long and drawn out as you get to the western border of Kansas. But Lopez and I played a game naming the cities and towns as we drove. It takes away the boredom of nothing but pavement.

Lopez and I really enjoyed the last part of our trip when we drove into the Springs on Highway Twenty Four. Suddenly we both felt good and full of life again. I have a whole list of things I want to do as soon as I get out of this car. I could go to the office, probably not. I could go home and see my family, wife and kids. That sounds good.

"I've been working on the design of our new patio and screenroom while you were gone. I think I have a few good ideas." Denise said.

"What did you come up with?"

"Here, take a look at it." She said.

She has a twelve by twenty-four room looking out and opening out onto a large concrete patio. The patio is about twenty-five feet square. It looks like a good design. It also looks expensive.

"Wow! This really looks good."

I gave it back to her. Now she will find out just how expensive it really is.

I made her a list of the guys I knew that were in construction.

"Be sure to contact Jason about the concrete. He is the best and I'm sure he will give you the best price. I don't know if he would do all of it, but you can always ask. I trust him"

Chapter 4

Two Girls

We have two women who were in distress and both landed in our laps. Neither Mike nor I know what to do about these two. I suggested that we flip for choice of them. But Mike decided he wanted Amber O'Reilly - because she was Irish.

Mike always seems to forget that he and I are both Irish when it's convenient for him. We have the same grandfather, we look like twins in size and facial features. I'm a better shot than he is. But if that's what he wants, it's OK with me.

That means that Lopez and I will have to transport Nema to Colorado Springs with us. Well if that's what it takes then that's what we'll do.

It looks like my little audio recorder will get another workout on the trip back home. I need to know everything about this girl and her family. Also work experience.

Mike always takes the easiest ones. Amber is a natural born American who had a problem with a stupid teacher who thought he was Mister America and could get away with anything he wanted to do.

I have a naturalized citizen who was not born in the US and may not know all the little niceties of living here.

Maybe I will get lucky and Denise and some of the other women in the city will take her under their wing and teach her what she needs to know.

During the long trip home, Nema told us a lot about the anti American groups in the Middle East. She knew names and places. She also knew addresses and she had a little black book full of everything imaginable.

The best part of that little book is that it has little identifiers for almost all of them. There were moles, scars, twitches, color and length of hair, facial hair, sometimes drawings. This was a gold mine.

When it was my turn to drive, I passed the book over to Lopez and he ate it like candy. He kept saying. "Wow, this is fantastic. There are names here I know or have heard."

"Well, let's go get them!"

"This one is in Massachusetts, this one is in New York, New Jersey, Ohio is the closest. We're going to need a lot of help. I'll call what's-his-name in the FBI when we get home. I don't know if we can help with these guys. They're so far away." He said.

"Hey! Here's one I know is in Colorado! I know we could get him! Here's another one!" Lopez really got fired up and his voice got louder when he found a couple names that he knew.

Then pretty soon Lopez found a name in New Mexico, then Utah, Wyoming, Kansas and Nevada.

"There are lots of names in Nevada, but most of them are in Las Vegas." He said. He sounded dejected then.

Over the years, we've got to know most of the agents, officers and officials in the west. I know because sometimes when I call they'll say, "Hey man, how you doin'? Heard you got one the other day. I got one last month."
Stuff like that.
Lopez assigned some of the clerks and typists to make a flier with questions and answers that we can hand out to the teachers. Explaining in detail the evil we are hunting.
The police flier has phone numbers and all the other things that people need to know how to tell us. We will investigate all leads, no matter how small. We made sure to get and give phone numbers of local police and others who will help.

I waited until we got back home and had a little down time in the office before I asked Lopez again.
"Where do you want to go on our next fishing expedition?"
"What did you have in mind, big fisherman?" He said.
"We could visit all the National Parks and Monuments and have a good time eliminating a lot of trouble."

"You know we would have to take a crew with us and Nema too. She might recognize them, speak their language, maybe tell us a clue on body language or a slip of the tongue." He said.

"Great idea!"

"The way the weather is here, we could go to Wyoming, Colorado and Utah in the summer and Arizona, New Mexico and Nevada in the winter. Spend spring and fall at home." He said.

"I like that! Let's do it!"

"We'll have to get volunteers. I wouldn't want to just arbitrarily assign someone to a job like this." He said.

Lopez and I talked about it every day. It didn't get any easier. We both think we should offer this as a volunteer assignment.

We went into the conference room and asked everyone to join us.

Lopez started. He explained what the plan was and as many details as possible. Then he asked for volunteers. To my surprise, every hand in the place was touching the ceiling.

"You do realize that this could be a very dangerous outing. We might invite some crazy to shoot at us. He could possibly hit someone."

"Yes, DJ he might. But that would make him an obvious target and someone here would level him." Paul said.

"Besides, you're the only one here who has been shot that we know about." Ann said.

"I'll take these two on my team." Then I pointed at them.

Everyone laughed. But I got another good one after that. Sergeant Zarif. He speaks and understands Arabic, but doesn't have the look.

After that, I took anyone who offered to come. I think I have as good a crew as Lopez does.

"OK. Everyone picked should pack for two weeks. We'll leave Monday morning." Lopez said.

Early Monday morning there was another emergency for us to deal with, but we'll get started soon.

I was outside studying the area Denise wanted to remodel, enjoying a Pepsi and trying to imagine how it would look, when Denise sat down beside me.

"I contacted Jason and the others. He said he would be here to look at it tomorrow. The others will try to get to me this week." She said.

"I'm beginning to get interested in your plan. I hope he will give you some good info."

A week later, Lopez and I took a crew to Wyoming and Utah to fish for teachers and administrators who are either terrorists or sympathetic to them.

Since Dave Wynn had been to Salt Lake before, I got Utah and Lopez got Wyoming. I think he got the easier part.

I have my favorite FBI guy on speed dial. If we find one we don't want to waste time in a holding pattern.

Lopez is going to start on the north-south route first then work toward Salt Lake to meet us.

I have called ahead to my Wyoming contact, Martin Butcher, and explained the plan. We met in Cheyenne. He introduced all of us to the Police Chief and all the people there.

"I don't get to this part of the country very often, but for him, I'll make an exception." He said as he pointed at me. "By the way, what is your name anyway?" He asked.

They all began to chuckle about that one.

"I am David Wynn when I'm in Utah, and I have taught Finance and Accounting at the University of Utah."

"Oh, yes, now I remember you. You are something of a troublemaker I understand." He said.

"Why, thank you. I didn't think you had noticed."

They all got several laughs out of his little game with me.

Everyone laughed and shook my hand and Martin told them some of the good things I have done. Few as they may be.

Lieutenant Lopez and his crew will be starting here in Wyoming, in Sheridan, then Buffalo, Gillette, Worland, Thermopolis, Casper, Douglas, Wheatland, and back to Cheyenne. Then the west road, to Laramie, Rawlins, Rock Springs, Green River, ending in Evanston. Then we'll meet in Salt Lake and go home.

We all talked for hours and spent the night. In the morning my crew and I were off toward the big city in Utah. It's a four hundred and fifty mile drive today, and we want to get there before dark.

I took Lopez aside and told him a few things I thought he should know.

"Don't forget to talk to the ROTC guys at the University of Wyoming in Laramie. They might be of some valuable help. If you want to see that big rock called the Devi's Tower, it's in the Black Hills north east of Gillette somewhere. And don't forget there are bears roaming all over the roads there. Be careful, they're strong and hungry. Don't feed them."

"I know all about the bears and the ROTC guys. We just might drive up to the big Park when we get to Gillette. See you in Salt Lake." He said.

Before we arrived in Salt Lake I wanted to remind my crew of something important.

"You all remember the job Jim and I had here in Salt Lake last year? Well my name when I'm here is David Wynn. My cover was as a teacher at the university, so please don't call me DJ."

As soon as we arrived, I went straight to the PD where I had been working out of before.

When we walked in, Lieutenant Ray Wright came over and spoke to me.

"What are you here for now, David?" He asked.

I explained what we were doing and they said they were glad to help. They even offered to send officers with us if we wanted.

"We're going to do all the big small towns and will end up in Salt Lake. We'll start in Logan, then Brigham City, Ogden, and Bountiful."

"Then go to Orem, and Provo, Nephi, Beaver, Cedar City, and St George. Then end up in Salt Lake. I kinda like Salt Lake."

"We'll be in constant contact with Lopez and his guys, on cell phones in case anyone needs help."

But the one thing all of them in the Salt Lake PD wanted to know was, "What did you do with the Woody?"

"I turned it over to Norm, our Chief Mechanic Genius. He and his crew restored it to like new condition. My wife drives it more than I do."

One guy said that he didn't think that was possible given the condition it was in.

"I didn't either, but Norm is a regular magician."

This was a good time to tell them all how they could get a car or truck from the Foundation. I tried to explain it as quickly as I could and told them to talk to Ray and get an application.

Lieutenant Ray wanted to take our two crews on an extended touristy tour of the city and surrounding area. I don't know where he got the bus, but the next day there was a bus sitting outside the PD. All of us piled in and Ray drove.

The tour included the Temple, the Tabernacle, and the Capitol Building before anything else. Then Fort Douglas, the University of Utah, the railroad station, and This is The Place. Of course we had to drive up to Snowbird. Boy I'm glad it's summer. I wouldn't want to drive up that road in this bus in the winter. But later, the stop for lunch was one of the best where I had ever eaten.

Our first stop was Orem. I'm so glad that we started there. It was just what I expected it to be. Calm, peaceful and no one telling us about terrorists and drug dealers.

You would not believe what we found in the little town of Nephi. While I was passing out fliers and talking to students, one of them came up to me and said this.

"There's a teacher in Civics that talks funny. I don't understand most of his ideas and illustrations. It sounds like he's off in his own world." He said.

Ann Webster was there with me when the student was explaining it. It only took a few minutes for Sergeant Webster to be directed to a teacher that several students said he talked like a terrorist.

My phone rang just then.

"I found one David! Notice that I got the name right. I'm heading toward the car with him and Sergeant Solano." Ann said.

"OK. I'll meet you there."

On the way to meet them, a student stopped me and asked a question.

"Your flier talks about terrorists. Is that all you guys are looking for?" My new friend said.

"We're always looking for anyone who would try to put our students in trouble. What have you got?"

"I know there's a kid here that sells drugs to any student with some money. I could show you who it is." He said.

"You bet! Let's go!"

He almost ran ahead of me to get to the right place. He stopped suddenly and pointed to a kid sitting on one of the benches in a small grassy clearing.

"I got this one, Thanks."

He took off running back away from the clearing. He didn't want to be seen when the action happened. I walked up behind the kid he identified. I reached into my shoulder holster to remove James Bond and presented myself to him.

"Hi there! Would you please stand up and put your hands behind your back for me?"

"What? No! Who are you?" He said.

"My name is One Shot McCoy, and this is James Bond, I waved it under his nose, and you are under arrest. If you come along peacefully, I won't have to shoot you."

That woke him up and and soon we were walking toward the car with one of my crew collecting him and escorting him to the car.

I got on the phone to the FBI and told them what we had. It wasn't long before we had company and the terrorist teacher and my drug dealer were on their way to Salt Lake for questioning. And probably some time in jail.

Beaver and Cedar City were as good as Orem, but we found a few interesting things in St. George.

The most fun was when we were directed to a guy working as a clerk in a hardware store, and I was just passing the time with him. I seem to have grown into asking my favorite question. So I said it.

"Where were you born?"

"Danbury, Kentucky." He said with a smile.

I couldn't help it. I had to laugh! They bring these people in here to try to undermine our country, and they can't even remember the most important lie they are supposed to tell.

"Don't you mean Danbury, Connecticut? There isn't a Danbury in Kentucky."

I could tell this bewildered him. The look on his face was so funny that I laughed again.

We arrested him and Ray did a thorough check on him. He was one of them. Big surprise! I'll tell Martin Butcher, my FBI guy, to have some fun with this one.

Now we go to Salt Lake for a week.

A few days later, one of Lopez's girls found a professor who corrupted a teacher. He convinced a teacher to give a job to one of his friends as a teachers assistant. He assured her that this person was eminently qualified. But that was a lie.

No one would have ever found out except that this teacher found a paper dropped by the professor that explained the truth. She slipped it to me when we were alone and put her finger to her lips in that motion that says, "be quiet." This letter was signed by a school board member in Santa Fe. Looks like someone will be going to New Mexico very soon. Lopez suggested that we stop there on the way home. He gets excited when we have chances like this.

Once we did the checks needed for this scam we let the teacher go. She was innocent and didn't need any more harassment,she was only trying to help another teacher.

The professor was a different story. They will pick up the professor as soon as they locate him. The professor is the guilty one, and we will gladly put him away just as soon as we can.

Now we need answers to a whole new group of questions. We need an explanation about how they got into the country. Who helped them? Probably other teachers, but which ones? Have we picked up the helpers yet? The big question is how did they get into the high places of authority?

I faxed the letter to my FBI guy and told him we might be able to meet him in Santa Fe soon. .

Chapter 5

Who's Teaching?

Lopez and I took a side trip through Santa Fe on the way back to the Springs. We asked a few questions and found the answer at the college. This professor was easy to find. He has been talking crazy for quite a while and we simply collected him and called our friends at the FBI to pick him up and take him somewhere.

The school board member was a little harder to find and shocked that we knew about him. He really wanted to resist, but Lopez put the arm on him and he sat right down. The FBI will get a lot of information out of him. I feel certain after listening to him for only a few minutes.

Those are the kind of deliveries that I like to make.

Last year we alerted all the towns on Interstate Seventy that they were in danger of the terrorist teachers and what they could look for to identify them. They have been bringing them in as fast as they can.

The following Monday, we all had a big meeting about teachers. Our people said that they found one in the Springs while we were gone. They sent him to the Colorado State Prison in Canon City.

The prison there looks a lot like Leavenworth. It might have been designed by the same architect.

Very large, Very imposing. I've been there. Glad I don't live there.

"He'll love it there if he can stay alive." One of the women said.

All of the people in the squad got together and arranged a meeting with teachers from various schools, administrators and the teachers union. They all have been talking about teachers who are espousing the hate speech in the name of 'free speech' to the students. Not teaching the right ways but the old wrong ways.

When I finally got the chance to speak, I told them about what I found while we were parading around the country.

"Listen, I found a state regulation that shows in great detail how to fire a teacher, no matter how much time that they have put in. I don't know which state, but most of them are probably the same. We'll use this one as long as we can. I'll make copies for each of you."

Of course all of them denied that any of this was their fault.

"We're not here to place blame, you are all at fault."

"We don't have terrorists in our schools." One of the senior administrators said. The Union Representative loudly agreed with him.

"Would you like to see proof? I can show you both living and dead proof."

There was a long silent pause.

"No? Well, I was right. I was sure you wouldn't want to see proof. That would mean that you weren't doing your job. I thought you wouldn't want anyone to show proof that you are hiring people without doing a background check on them. I have people tell me that they think you are working with the terrorists."

"Maybe you are! Prove me wrong!"

"Do you know how many professors we found who were born in Yemen, or Somalia, or Iran who are now, this very minute, in a college classroom telling your children to hate America and anyone who lives here who does not agree with them? And that they should kill them." I paused for effect.

"Oh! You didn't know that?" I paused again and drew a big breath. "There is one thing more that you need to know. If you don't clean house, we will! And it won't be pretty!"

I stood up and walked out and down the hall to Lopez's office for a cup of coffee.

After a few minutes, I snuck back down the hall and tried to listen to the conversation.

I heard a female voice saying, "There's nothing worse than a teacher who hates people. Very bad."

Then another, "There's nothing worse than a teacher who hates children. Worse than that."

Then a male voice. "There's nothing worse than a teacher that hates this country. Worse than that."

Then a big male voice. "There's nothing worse than a teacher that hates God." Worst of all."

I recognized that voice. Good for him.

"One of the girls in dispatch yelled out. "DJ! Phone!"

I picked it up as she yelled "Line two!"

"Hello. This is DJ."

"Hold on sir, the Speaker would like to talk with you." A female voice said.

"Hello One Shot, this is Chuck Johnson. I have urgent need of your services. And could you bring Ted and be sure to fly that beautiful blue plane. I told a couple of friends about it and they really want to see it." He said.

"Do you know that we just returned from Indianapolis and haven't had any time with the family?" I said. "OK, now tell me what you really want us to do, and don't lie or shade the truth. Just tell me straight out so I can be prepared and prepare the rest of them."

He told me. Just the facts. Now I have to get together with the rest of the guys and make a plan.

"Yes, and now you get to see the great city named after our first President of this magnificent country". He said.

"Boy, you sure are full of it today. I'll bet this job of yours is going to be dangerous and no fun for anyone, especially me."

"I wouldn't say 'No fun'. I know you pretty well and I am sure this will be lots of fun for you. How soon can you get here. How about the first of the month?" He said.

"I'll call Ted and we won't try very hard to make it by the first, so don't count on it. But maybe with some incentive, we might. Where would we keep the plane if we did come to your wonderful city?"

"I have that all taken care of. Just land at that little airport in Silver Springs and we'll pick you up. What kind of incentive?" He said.

"Sounds like you've got this all worked out. Oh, you'll think of something. Maybe I'll call you when we're ready to leave, but don't count on it. By the way who buys the fuel for Big Blue?"

"You do of course. You're the one with all the money." He chuckled a lot when he said that.

"Well Mister Speaker, I will talk to Ted and we won't try very hard to make your meeting. But no funny stuff. I remember what you did to me the last time we were there."

"Oh, come on. You and your folks came out very well." He said.

"And I suppose that Ted and I will come out very well this time too?"

He avoided answering that last question.

"There's a little airport in Silver Springs, you can land there and we will pick you up and drive to the Big House, I will have the Press Secretary, Jerry Vernon, meet you there and take you wherever you need to go. You'll like him." He said.

I called Mike and Ted and the Lieutenants and filled everyone in on what the Speaker and I had talked about. All of them said that they were on board with it all.

I was anxious to talk to Denise. As much as I didn't want to spend thousands on our house, we will probably stay in this house from now on. It makes sense to do it right.

"Hello." Denise said.

"Hi Denise, it's me."

"Oh DJ, I'm so glad you called. I hired Jason to do the concrete and it's almost done. But better yet. He came up with some ideas to make the whole project better." She said.

"What did he do?"

"We don't get a lot of rain, but when we do it comes all at once. So we put down four inch sewer tile under the concrete and will have the downspouts from the roof drain right into them. The water will run out to the alley and then to the storm drain nearby." She said.

"What a great idea!"

"Another thing. He drew up an outdoor kitchen on the patio. I love it! It will have a propane cooktop, a single bowl sink and a little fridge. So he ran the wiring and plumbing before the pour." She said.

"It sounds better every time I hear from you. Keep up the good work. Love you."

Chapter 6

Back to Work

It was lot of work getting things done in Washington, but we all got lucky and Lopez and I feel pretty good about it.

Our priorities suddenly changed once we were on the ground in Falcon and our wives were there to meet us. I don't care how much fun that big blue plane is, traveling takes it out of you!

Every time I get back to town, I do want to see Norm about the Foundation cars. Denise and Lopez wanted to see too. He always seems to have a certain diamond in the rough hidden in the back with the wrecks. My second stop is to see Earl. He'll probably have something that he needs help with.

We have given away hundreds of cars and trucks. Some new, some old, but all renewed and running. The best part is that Norm finds the diamonds every so often. That's how we got the Ranchero for Jim. Norm rebuilt that '41 Ford Woody Wagon for me, but that wasn't the oldest or the newest car he found.

Dee and I are walking very slowly around the shop. I feel sure there is one here somewhere. I can always tell by Norm's body language.

"OK, Norm, I give up. I can't find anything, but I know there's another fancy car here. You wouldn't be acting like this if there wasn't. I've known you too long."

"It's been here right in front of you the whole time." He said.

Norm lifted a cover off of a car not ten feet away and showed me a showroom condition 1952 Ford Custom. It had the whole ball of wax. From full size wheel covers and white wall tires, to custom leather seats and a 239 cubic inch V-8 engine. All dressed up in a Cadillac looking rich dark green.

"I had a '54 like this a long time ago but it was not nearly as nice as this. Mine was worth a few hundred. I'll bet this one is ten times that."

"More like thirty or forty times." He said.

"Has anyone claimed it?"

"Everyone who sees it wants it, but most of them don't qualify. They all have nice cars and houses and enough money to buy it, and that's not what we do." Norm said.

"Right!"

"How's your flying going?" He said.

"I just got back from to DC, and Ted did all the flying and I just sat there and enjoyed it. I think I'm going to let him do it all from now on."

"What is in DC?" He asked.

"A leaker of secrets."

"Is that all?" He asked.

"This one is important!"

"They say everything is important." Dee said.

"Nothing now, but I'll bet they call us again and want us to fix something new. There was some counterfeit there, but I'm sure that's been taken care of by now. We shouldn't need to go again for a long time. We'll go to New Mexico next."

"Let's talk about it Monday in the office." Lopez said.

Lopez had all the crew in the conference room as I walked in. I just made it.

"We'll have to divide up the New Mexico trip into three parts, too. One group could start in Santa Fe and follow I 25 all the way down to El Paso." Lopez said.

"One of the other teams would have to take the back roads from Las Vegas south along 84 and 54. But you have a bonus. White Sands is right there at Alamogordo."

"The other team would have to take US 285 from that place just outside of Santa Fe and follow it through Roswell and Carslbad then back through the desert to El Paso." He said.

"I'll take that one. And of course, we will have to stop and go through the famous Carlsbad Caverns.'

Well, just like Lopez said, we split up into three squads and I got the back-road one. We had fewer towns, but a lot more fun and interesting landscapes. He started in Raton and followed I25 all the way south to Las Cruces.

But my crew cut off at Las Vegas then we cut in half at Vaughn. Half went toward Roswell and half toward White Sands. I've been to Alamogordo, so I stayed with the Roswell group. The only problem was the dreary drive from Carlsbad through the desert to El Paso.

But we got the Carlsbad Caverns. What an experience that was. It's dark and the path that you take is lit up with tiny little lights in the ground. There was so much to see we could have gone through it several times and not got it all.

We don't usually have a chance to talk to our other teams, but I had to call Ted about a strange idea I got in the middle of the night.

"Hey Ted, I have a funny idea that might help locate some of these terrorist teachers and leakers. What if we took DNA from everyone and sorted out the ones from the countries that are trying to kill us. Then we might have a lot better chance of getting close to the right ones."

"You might finally have a good idea." He said with a huge smile creeping all over his face. He took out his pen and paper and began to make notes. Well it's about time he recognized my budding genius.

Anytime I arrive in Albuquerque, I am going to make it a point to see Gene Di Angelo. He and I worked together for ten years before he got transferred. And I haven't seen him since.

Gene came to the door and saw me and said, "Hey, man! How ya doin'?" He grabbed me and we shook hands and patted backs like we were old friends, which we are.

"You still Plum Crazy?"

"You bet! We have three of them now. And my wife and kids love to ride too!" He said.

Gene built a VW Karmann Ghia into a sand buggy that would almost fly. Then he painted it a bright metallic purple and named it 'Plum Crazy'. He invited me in and we talked and had coffee for a few minutes.

"You still working?" He asked.

I shook my head yes as I took another drink.

"Whadda ya do." He asked.

I showed him my badge and he stopped talking, but his mouth was open.

"Really?" He said. "OK! Whadda ya do?"

We sat down and I told him all that I do without breaking any secrets or confidences. He was surprised to say the least.

"I've been with them for a long time now. Ever since you left the team."

"You wouldn't believe it but I get to shoot drug dealers." I laughed at that one.

"Wow! I've got so many questions, I don't know where to start." He said.

We sat where no one could hear us whisper and I gave him a skeletons view of what I do. He was shocked but, he still had questions, but they will have to wait.

"Remember all this is secret and you still have a clearance. If you need to contact me, my alias for this state is Bob Pessetto. I'll respond quickly if you use it."

After we were done talking, I met his wife and family and it was time to go back to work.

"I guess I'll see you the next time I get to the Queen City."

I hurried to meet Lopez and the rest of the crew so we could get started back home to the Springs.

Denise is always my first call when I get on the ground in the Springs.

"Oh, DJ, I'm so glad you called. I've missed you and so have the kids."

"Jason finished the subfloor on the room, and put down the plywood floor and all the walls are up and he's working on the shingles right now. He is everything you said he would be. The roof will be done soon and the walls will be insulated." She said.

"Maybe you won't have to do much of the work after all." She said.

"Good!"

Chapter 7

Press Conference

It was a long drive home and I was dragging when I found the door to my house. I moved quietly inside and put my bags down. That couch looks so inviting. Oh, yes. This is nice. I think I'll just lay here for a minute.

"DJ! Get up!"

Denise is shaking me. "What's going on?"

"It's almost noon. What time did you get home?" She asked.

"Huh? What?"

I sat up and she hugged me. It took a minute to get on track. She decided that I should go upstairs and start from the beginning as if I just woke up. Good idea.

It took me some time but I finally got myself ready for work. But this is Saturday and we don't need to be in the office till Monday. What a relief. Denise made me something to eat and the kids all had questions about what I did this time and where did I go.

So I started from the beginning and we all talked and ate and enjoyed the weekend.

"While you were gone this time, Jason finished all the electrical and the plumbing work for the downspouts. The room is completely insulated and the sheetrock is finished. It looks like a room now."

"Great! Let's go see it."

"It's supposed to rain today at two o'clock. I hope we get to see how well the sewers work." She said.

Sure enough. At two o'clock the rain clouds blew in from the west and we got a big shower. Me, my crazy wife and kids all ran out to the alley in the rain to see if everything worked the way she wanted it. It did! They loved it!

The Speaker called again this evening and I could hear him demanding, pleading, begging for us to get this problem solved.

"OK, OK! We'll fly out tomorrow."

The Speaker was right about one thing. Ted loved the idea and said it was another chance for him to get to fly the big blue plane.

I knew there would be people crawling all over me, so I put on one of my small masks that I can wear for a few hours. I don't want photos of me anywhere. And whadda you know! I was right. There were reporters and photographers swarming all around when the car went to the Capitol even before the car stopped.

I don't know how they knew or found out that someone different was coming to the Big House, but there they are. Screaming and yelling and acting stupid. It looks like a demonstration against one of the million things that they hate. I guess I'm one of them.

They don't know my name. They took photos of me in my mask, and didn't know it. They didn't get to hear my voice. They don't know if I'm a foreigner. And especially, they don't know if I'm important or not. But they still act stupid.

They shoved microphones in my face but I gave them no response. Not one word. Boy that makes them mad. I always thought that was funny. Wait till tomorrow, when the mask is changed but they don't know it.

Jerry led me to a room where the meeting was to take place. I met his assistant, some Senators and Congressmen, and lots of aides.

Before Ted and I entered, Jerry stood up and said. "Attention! There will be no microphones, no cameras, no video recorders, no press people, and no phones allowed in this room until we are released from this meeting. If you have one of these things, you may hand it to my assistant or you may leave."

That little announcement caused quite a stir. Several people turned in their electronics, and several were forced to leave. The latter were very unhappy.

The Speaker began by telling us about a big problem in DC that no one seemed to be able to handle. He said that was the reason he brought Ted and I in to work on it.

He finally got down to the meat of the meeting.

"We have a huge problem developing here with counterfeit money. One Shot and Ted solved this problem in Kansas City a few years ago and that is why I have called them in. They have a crew of knowledgeable people and I am going to ask them to rid our fair city of this plague." He said.

Unfortunately that was my cue.

"Mr. Speaker, I know that is not the reason we are here. This stuff is so easy that all your SS guys can do it with their eyes closed. What is the real reason that you called us?"

"Well, we are having trouble containing the leaks that seem to come out of nowhere." He said.

"Now we're getting somewhere! Could everyone talk about specific instances where a leak happened? We will make notes and would appreciate if you could write down anything you have."

We had a long discussion and everyone had some evidence and ideas but nothing concrete.

We will get back to the money problem, but this is far more important and we haven't been briefed on anything relating to the counterfeiting as yet.

Ted and I didn't have any good ideas right then, but we will spend the rest of the morning talking to everyone in the room and make notes. I think we should be able to piece something together.

Later that afternoon, we began again with the money.

"Also, One Shot and his friends have taught classes on all sorts of finance, counterfeiting and money laundering several times in the past." The Speaker said.

I wish he would stop adding little niceties here and there and let us listen to the people he has invited to this meeting.

"Can you show us how to easily recognize a counterfeit bill from a real one?" One Congressman asked.

"Yes. I can do that in only a few minutes. But I will need a magnifying glass and some paper money."

Jerry had a magnifying glass in his briefcase and all the rest produced paper money to be examined.

I went through the steps of discovering the lines and marks on the various bills to show them the basic ideas of the bills. We finally found one bad bill.

"Well, finally! I have a counterfeit twenty dollar bill. Whose is this?"

One Senator stepped up. "That one is mine, unfortunately." He said.

"Do you know where you received this bill? I hope it was from a bank. That would make things a lot easier."

He tried to think about the question and said, "I think it might have been a bank close to my home."

"Let's go for a ride. Ted can show the rest of you more details and we'll be back as soon as we can." I said to the class.

We hurried out to the Senator's parking place and the Senator's assistant jumped into the drivers seat and we were off.

It was a long drive across town to where the Senator lived and then to the bank he used. I asked them to wait in the car so they wouldn't be recognized with me. I'm an unsavory character and I didn't want it to rub off on the Senator or his aide.

I walked to the first teller that was available and said, "Good afternoon, ma'am. May I have change for these? Would you mind giving me twenties?" I handed her two one hundred dollar bills.

She counted out ten twenty dollar bills and slid them out to me under the glass.

"Thank you." I said and briskly left the building.

Once I was back in the car I pulled out the magnifying glass and examined each one of the bills.

"I found one!"

I was smiling broadly and they were wondering what was wrong with me.

"Let's get back. I have a lot of work to do."

I wrote down the name and address of the bank and folded everything up and hid it in my pocket.

The aide drove us back to the meeting and I told the Speaker and Ted what we found.

I felt pretty good about my very first meeting with the big hot politicians and Ted. I was basking in the glow and quietly and slowly walking down the hall toward the 'OUT' door when Jerry came along side of me and he stopped me for a minute to talk.

Just as he was starting, another aide ran up to us and said that the President wanted to see him. It was urgent. He looked at me and I died inside.

"Here! Take care of this would you?" He said. And he shoved a big handful of papers into my hands.

Like I had a choice.

Jerry ran down the hall and I asked the aide where did I need to go for this mess. The aide led me through a couple doors and into the Press Room.

I walked into the briefing room and took my place behind the podium.

"Good morning, ladies and gentlemen. You don't know me so you may call me 'Sir'. I don't have a name."

One of the guards stepped to the front and said, "Would George Jones come to the rear for a phone call?"

I had asked one of the guards to do this George Jones thing to see if they would bite on it. And they did.

Five Georges showed up. All were cuffed and arrested. Ted and I will examine them. Each of them had a press card with their name, and the media they represented.

"I will be handling the briefing today. These are the rules of the day. If you want to speak, you will raise your hand and I will point at you. I don't know any of your names here so this will make it a lot simpler for you."

A man in the second row jumped up and said, in a loud voice. "Wait just a minute! You can't do that! Who do you think you are anyway?" He was carrying a camera and snapping pix as fast as he could.

"Guard! Remove this man and take his pass. I did not point at him and he was not given permission to speak. And I don't take sass from anyone, least of all a creepy reporter who writes lies in all his articles. I've read some of them, and I know what the truth is!

Don't forget to check him for weapons and remove that camera from him."

"if it was up to me, I'd put him in jail, but I don't get to have any fun sometimes."

"Before you take him away, maybe I should tell him and all of you folks, who I am. The guards all know me and we have worked together several times. I am called One Shot McCoy".

Off to the side we heard one of the Georges say "Oh, no!" in a loud voice.

"Well, I see I have a fan there on that side."

All the reporters turned and looked. All the George Jones' were being held there.

"How is it that you know my name George?"

I was told that you were the one who killed my crew in Kansas City." He said.

"And who would that be?"

"They called themselves The Store Front Gang." He said.

"Oh yes. I remember them, they weren't very smart. One of them wanted to show how he could take over the city but James Bond told him different. By the way, cousin Jim helped me on that little exciting hunting trip. He enjoyed it too."

"James Bond? What has he got to do with it?" He asked.

I reached in and pulled out my nine millimeter friend, JB, and showed him. All the reporters were shocked and made that sound when they inhaled loudly.

"Did you think that we walk around without some form of deterrent in our hand? I never know when one of you will attack me or some citizen. I am prepared to stop you twenty four hours a day."

"Did you people think that I was some kind of reporter or press person? You couldn't pay me enough to do that!"

The guard took the camera from the big mouth reporter and led the man out of the room. The man was complaining all the way, saying he was important and should be shown some respect. Funny how the ones who deserve the least respect, say that they should have the most, but they always have a loud mouth. The ones who actually deserve the respect usually are quiet and reserved, and are quietly given the respect they deserve.

The place calmed down after that. We started again and I pointed to a woman in the fourth row.

"Yes sir. I have two questions for you, is that OK?"

"Yes ma'am, please continue."

"First, where is the Press Secretary today, and will you be handling the briefings from now on?" She said.

"I was minding my own business walking down the hall with Jerry, when a man ran up to us and said he had an urgent call from the President. Jerry shoved all this paper into my hands and said, 'Take care of this would you', and ran down the hall."

"So here I am, for now. I don't know about 'from now on'. I will probably become invisible again once this conference is over. I only do as I am told minute by minute."

"I do know one thing. That reporter picked the wrong guy to mess with. He wouldn't like me when I'm angry."

The guards were told to read and examine all the press cards and give any that looked funny to me. There were more than one that said George Jones. I told my closest guard to apprehend and cuff all of them. But the best one of the day was a guy named Little Big Town. I couldn't help it, but I had to laugh.

"Little Big Town, would you please come up here."

A man near the rear stood up and approached the front where I was standing.

"According to this card, your name is Little Big Town. Is that correct?"

"Yes."

I chuckled at the name and the man using it. There was a little chuckling in the room, too.

"How is it that you have the name of a famous country music group?"

"I don't understand." He said.

Oh, boy. I can see this is going to be good! I'll bet that there isn't anyone in this country over twenty that doesn't know that LBT is a country singing group. This guy is a foreigner, probably a terrorist.

"Your first name is Little. Is that right?"

I can't help it, but I began to smile and chuckle when he first said the name and now I'm losing it.

"Yes, sir." He said. More chuckling. I couldn't help it.

"And your middle name is Big?"

"Yes sir." He said. More chuckling.

"And your last name is Town. So far I'm right on all three, is that right?"

"Yes sir. I am a member of the Town family." He said.

Downright laughing out loud now from all around the room.

"Funny, but you don't look like a quartet. And those two beautiful girls will be surprised when they see your picture. I don't know them, but I'll have someone send these photos to them. I'm sure they will get a few laughs out of them. Just like the people in this room."

By this time the whole room was laughing and holding there mouths and stomachs.

"Do you have a press pass?"

"Yes sir." He said, and handed it to me.

"It says here that you are a reporter for one of the local Washington newspapers. Is that correct?"

"Yes sir." He said. He never smiled at anything that was said. I wonder if he is really serious about this.

"Have you ever interviewed anyone in the music industry."

I couldn't help myself. It is just too funny. I continued to ask him about his job, and he gave me what sounded like 'canned' answers. So I tried the favorite question of all.

"Let me start again with an easier question. Where were you born?"

I leaned over to the guard and said. "If he says Danbury, Connecticut we've got him."

"Danbury, Connecticut." He said.

"We need to take him to Belle View and get everything we can from him. He's just crazy enough that he might tell the doctors there some important news." I said to the guard.

I motioned to one of the guards in the back of the room, who took him in hand and led him out the door. The room broke into raucous laughter at that time and continued until I went back to the podium.

I'm sure glad Jerry left all those papers with me. I didn't know the answers to any of the questions that they asked, but I found most of them hidden in the paperwork. The rest of the press conference went well and as soon as the last question was answered, I ran out the door and out a side door to the parking area.

Luckily, I wasn't followed. I always carry a small mask or parts of a disguise in my back pockets. As I walked, I suddenly changed into an interested tourist and walked around to the front door as fast as I could.

As I walked in the door I met the Press Secretary and Ted and told them who I was and filled him on the events of the day. He recognized my voice and he began to laugh as I started and continued to laugh even after I finished.

"He said he was Little Big Town?" He laughed as he said it.

"I wonder why he picked such an unusual name for a single guy?" He said.

"Maybe everyone here is as crazy as he is."

"You don't like Washington very much, do you DJ?" He asked.

"No.   And I hope I'm not called to come again before I retire."

"I bet you don't get laughs like this back home." That started him laughing again.

"I've got to find a plane or bus or train that is going my way. Especially a plane. A blue plane. Lopez must miss me. I certainly miss the home place."

"The Speaker would like to see you right away." He said.

Oh, man! Here we go again. Jerry took us to the Speaker's office.

"Could you and Ted step into my office and I will go over what I had in mind?' The Speaker said.

Ted and I followed him to a very nice huge office covered with wood where there were upholstered chairs, a fancy wood desk and a few side chairs for the underlings.

"I have been watching your progress for the last year or so. You don't like terrorists or drug dealers, I hear." He said.

"That is correct. We don't usually ask for help in collecting them."

"Well, I don't like counterfeiters, and I would like you to clean all of them out of this town. Just for me." Then he smiled that TV smile that he does.

"There you go again. You know we will help you, but there are a lot more nosy reporters here than where we are used to. I will not allow my identity to be found out! If the reporters find out who I am, I might as well quit. Every crook we have ever talked to would be gunning for me and my family."

"Is there that many that you would worry about it?" He asked.

"I could look it up for you if you want, Mister Speaker." Ted said.

Ted sat at the computer and began his finger tapping and within a few minutes he asked, "Does this number look nearly correct to you sir?"

"You're kidding! One Shot McCoy has shot and killed this many criminals?" He said. "I had no idea!"

I thought it was time for me to get into the conversation. "What do you want us to do about this?"

"I am going to get you a new identity while you are in Washington. Give me a couple days. Jerry has your reservations in a nice hotel here in town. I'll call him. You can hide out or whatever you want until I contact you." He said."

He called Jerry and we went to the hotel and checked in as George Brooks and Alan Atkins. It seems that we both like country singers.

For the last two days, Ted and I really had a good time while we laid around in one of the best hotels in town. We had fancy meals in the cafeteria and the fancy restaurant and even had some delivered up to the room. But I knew it had to end. Jerry called and told us that the Speaker was ready to unload on, uh, speak to us.

Jerry picked us up at nine in the morning and delivered us to a private meeting room. This one was a lot smaller than the first one and a whole lot less people attending.

Jerry gave us a heads-up on our name change on the way back from the hotel before we were introduced to the meeting.

"DJ will be Warren Martin and Ted will be Fred Williams." Jerry said quietly, almost as a whisper.

The Speaker stood and began his talk.

"We need a lot more cooperation between the federal officials and the states in this matter."

"I would like to introduce Warren Martin and Fred Williams. They will be heading up this investigation. We have all talked about this problem here in Washington. We must get a handle on it and these two will be doing that."

"As I have said before, Warren and Fred have worked on all facets of the financial business when it comes to crooks and their ideas. This includes counterfeiting, money laundering and terrorists trying to subvert our economy."

"They will have clearances to any building and room in every building in the city."

"In this case, they could be from the Federal Reserve, maybe inspectors. They would have access to all money in every bank. If there were counterfeit or money laundering going on, they could easily go into vaults and test all the currency."

"The second most important problem has to do with teachers, school administrators, left wing radicals, KKK, radical college kids, on and on."

"I'm afraid to ask, but what do you want us to do about that?"

"I have half a dozen men working on exactly that problem right now. I will get with you as soon as I have some good ideas. In the meantime, we will work on the money." He said.

Ted and I excused our selves and had Jerry take us back to the hotel. Both of us wanted to talk to our wives and get a bite to eat and plan our next few moves. Ted and I both need to talk to Denise and Vonnie just to get our perspective on straight.

Chapter 8

A Page 2 Story

The next day when I opened the door to go down to the cafeteria for breakfast, a newspaper was laying at the door. I picked up the paper and continued on my way. I was half through with my eggs and ham when Ted arrived and gave the waitress his order.

"Wait till you see this Ted."

I had the paper open to page two and handed it over to him.

The headline read, "Little Big Town Arrested!"

Ted read the article and had that look on his face when someone is surprised about an unbelievable event.

"It's a lie! You remember I told you about the crazy man we sent to Belle View? Well, he kept telling everyone that his name was Little Big Town. He is obviously a terrorist, because he told me about Danbury. And did you read all this LBT craziness? I'm going to that newspaper and it's not going to be pleasant. You want to go?"

"No. I better stay away from this one." Ted said and turned on the TV and the first news I heard was this big story from the WH.

"Little Big Town caused a commotion yesterday in the White House press room and was arrested and taken to Belle View for mental evaluation and is being held there." The TV reporter said.

"I wonder if the reporter was smiling as he wrote it."

I could feel the heat coming and I rushed out to cool off before I went to that newspaper office. Right now I could shoot someone there, but I was smiling.

I told Jerry about the article in the paper and what I wanted to do about it. He said I should calm down, but he did offer to give me a ride there.

The Washington Gazette Telegraph was only a short ride away. I told Jerry not to worry, I would try not to shoot anyone, but I didn't promise anything and I said that I was calm now.

The article in the paper had the reporter's name on it, so it was an easy search to find the right one.

"Are you Eugene Hicks?"

"Yes I am. What can I do for you?" He asked.

"I would like to talk to you about this Page Two story about someone taken to Belle View. Did you have a government source on it?"

"Well, yes. A guy called me and told me all about it over the phone." He said.

"Do you know who the guy is?"

"No, but I can remember his voice. It was very unusual." He said.

"Do you know who Little Big Town is?"

"No. Why? Should I?" He said.

This guy doesn't even know who he's writing about, or the source of the information, but he has lied and slandered them all through this article. I'm beginning to like this. I might get to shoot someone after all.

"We need to go visit the editor."

"But we can't go into his office." He said.

"I have a very special key!" I opened my jacket and introduced him to Jame Bond.

He started to shake a little when he saw it, but he stood up and headed for the office.

When we entered the office without knocking, the man behind the desk jumped up and said, "Hey! You can't come in here!"

"This says I can!" I introduced him to James Bond as well and he sat down in his chair. When he calmed down, I showed him my badge, just a quick look, not an examination.

"Now then! I am here to tell you the rules! You two have written and published a big lie! I know it is a lie because I was there. And I don't like it! I don't like to be involved in your lies. Now I am going to tell you what you are going to do to fix the problem!"

"You can't tell us how to run this business!" The editor said.

"Maybe not, but if you refuse I will have James Bond speak to you and you won't like what he says."

"Now let's start at the beginning. This clown of a reporter took a call from someone he doesn't know and wrote an article lying about one of the most famous country music groups in this country. He accused them of being arrested and taken to Belle View for mental evaluation. Do you know what the best part is? YOU! You put it on page two with a big headline."

"Is this true, Eugene?" He said. "Did you write that headline?"

"Well sort of. I didn't know who Little Big Town was and they said that was what this guy said his name was." Eugene said.

"You didn't think that Little was an unusual first name for a man?' And Big was his middle name?

"I guess I didn't think about that." He said.

"You just didn't think! It's time to start! We have changed his name to George Jones. We have already arrested five George Jones'. One more won't matter. None of them sing."

"Now that you two know the problem, I will tell you what the solution is. Tomorrow there will be an equally big story about a man who entered the White House and said he was Little Big Town and caused a commotion. He was then arrested by the White House police and held pending further action. He did not sing, he was not a country music group or any part of one, and the real Little Big Town members had no part in your phony story of yesterday."

"But we have the first amendment!" The editor said.

"Not when you knowingly lie and slander the good name of someone for profit. And you did make me angry. You wouldn't like me when I'm angry. You did sell more papers from this story, didn't you?"

He looked thoughtfully at his monitor for a minute and said. "Why, yes. Our circulation is up by twenty-five percent today. Oh dear! What have we done? This could be bad." The editor said.

"Don't forget! The retraction will be on the front page above the fold! Or else!"

"We can't do that!" He said.

"If you don't, I will be back here tomorrow with James Bond to speak to you. Oh by the way, if you don't believe me, you should call the Press Secretary or the Speaker of the House. They both know who I am and and what I can do."

"But I promise you. If you don't get this cleaned up today, there will be a lawyer removing you from this building."

"You only have a few choices, you could lie about it, you might not do anything, or you could pass it off to the higher ups."

"If these are your choices, I can reserve a room for you right next to the LBT guy over at Belle View. And don't think I can't. You wouldn't like me when I'm angry. Angrier than I am already."

"But, who are you?" He said.

"Just say One Shot McCoy was here."

He was on the phone before I got out the door.

Jerry stopped me as I walked in the front door. "What have you been doing? I got the funniest call from the editor of the GT, asking about you. I think you scared the crap out of him. There was another voice in the background. Do you know who that was?"

"Jerry, Jerry, Jerry. I only went to the newspaper to explain what they should do about their erroneous story on page two and tell them how to fix it."

"He said that you threatened them and said that you would shoot them." He said.

"I promise I won't do anything until I read the paper tomorrow. Honest." I said. "Then I'll shoot them." I laughed at my own joke, but Jerry was still scowling.

I don't know who is delivering the paper to our door or why, but I heard it hit the floor at six forty-one in the morning. I'm anxious to see what my little talk with those two will do.

Just like I told them, it was on the front page above the fold. A nice long story about how someone, who did not work for the GT, gave them a wrong story and told them it was true. Their retraction almost sounded honest.

Before I venture out into the cold of our Capital, I'll have some eggs and coffee and other stuff. I want to get started right. Jerry joined me just as the waitress brought the coffee. I saw that Jerry also enjoyed my idea of starting the day right.

I told Jerry that someone leaked the story to a reporter at the GT. This reporter said the he could identify the guys voice. I'm going to get him here to listen to voices and pick out the right one.

"Could you have a fake meeting and I'll bring this guy in by accident and maybe we might find our leak. This will be bad if it is someone close to us. I'm going to get him now, my driver is waiting."

It wasn't very long before we all returned to the White House. I walked in with Eugene and I had prepped him on what I wanted him to do.

Everyone was talking as we walked down the hall, and Eugene's ears perked up.

"I hear it." He said. "He is in here." He pointed toward a room off the hall.

As we entered the room, they all stopped talking and turned to us.

"Go on with what you were doing, we're just going to find a seat."

There were two seats in the back of the room.

"There it is again. On that side of the room." He said and pointed again.

"OK. Just one more time."

"The third guy down on this side. I'm sure of it" He said.

I stood up and said. "Well folks, we have identified our classified information leak. You there." I pulled James Bond from his resting place, and I pointed to him. "The third man sitting on this side. Would you stand, please."

I hurried to him. "Badge and gun please. I'll need some handcuffs, guys."

Two guys jumped up and grabbed the gun and put the cuffs on.

I looked at his ID and read the name off aloud.

"Omar Arabi, you are under arrest for espionage."

"It's no wonder we couldn't find the leak, it was right under our nose." Jerry said.

"You're not very funny with the puns, Jerry."

"You're not going to kill me. I'm a US Government employee and I have rights." He said.

"Not any more! You gave up those rights when you gave up the secrets that were uttered in this building."

"Now let me explain what I plan to do with you. There are a few options."

I smiled and rubbed my hands together. I could tell he didn't believe me, so I continued. This is starting to be fun.

There was a light chuckle in the room.

"I have been doing this for a long time. Years ago when I was a kid, there was an older boy who delighted in following Ted and I home from school and pounding us with his fists. We got tired of that pretty fast and Ted found a man who taught us all the ways to kill a person. In addition he taught us a lot of ways to hurt a man so bad that he would wish he were dead. Let me show you one."

I pulled out James bond again and pointed it at his crotch. He immediately covered it with his hands.

"Oh goodie! I get two hands as a bonus in this shoot."

There was a little chuckling before, but now it's becoming more often.

"This was just an easy one."

I'm still holding James bond and acting like I might use it.

"Now you have a few choices. First I could find something in my wide range of defensive fun to do to you. Or I could turn you over to these guys."

They all said that they would love that.

"Or." I paused for effect. "I have some friends who have a little hotel in a small town just a few miles north of Kansas City. I could reserve a room for you there and you could live there for a long time."

"What little town is that?" He asked.

"It's a surprise. I'll make the arrangements if that's what you choose."

"Yes, yes. I would rather take that." He said.

That brought many smiles among the others standing around the room.

"Check him for recording devices and put him somewhere where he won't talk to anyone, guys."

"We have a lot of work to do. But now we have one clue to the problem, look who hired him. The last administration, he's from Chicago. The guy that hired him lied, as usual. We need to clean out the trash."

This guy didn't want to be a tattle tale, but that was what he was hired for and he was fulfilling the role. His big problem was that now he is on the hook and the ones that gave him the job are getting away with it. They think! All of us have a few surprises for them.

They all smiled and hurried to get started on the cleanup, The room emptied in a few seconds.

Omar has told us the he heard that people want to kill him, he had been getting death threats. Well he'll be safe from that where he is going.

Jerry called the Speaker and asked him to come to the room. We all explained that we knew now that

Omar was found out. He gave us a few names of employees who he thought were doing the same thing. It didn't take long for all the guys to round up several left-overs who were making trouble. They will be joining Omar in our special hotel.

The Speaker was over-joyed. He kept telling each of the crew how much he liked them every day after that. He must have shook my hand a hundred times. Maybe not.

I contacted a Lawyer recommended by someone in the West Wing to sue the paper for LBT for slander.

The lawyer told the owner of the GT, "We will take a check from you for one million dollars made out to the St. Jude Children's Hospital, and we will drop all charges."

It could have been a long trial. The paper would have brought witnesses, the judge would not have believed them. It could have been messy. The reporter lied about his source, because some one threatened him. We found out who that was. Too bad for him.

After the hearing, the Washington GT agreed to pay Little Big Town a million dollars to be donated to the St. Jude Children's Hospital. I made a special trip to talk to the additional offending TV stations. I must be getting better. They each agreed to send an equal amount of money to Children's Hospital, and I didn't even threaten them.

That was really fun but I didn't get to shoot one guy. Too bad.

After all the legal mumbo jumbo was over, I called a well known reliable TV reporter and told him who the leaker was and that he has been arrested, convicted and sentenced to live in a little town north of Kansas City, on the Kansas side.

"What little town is that?" He asked.

"What do you mean you don't know what little town? Get a map or get off of the TV news."

He hung up on me. I don't do well with reporters.

I called another TV station and talked to another reporter who knew what little town it was, and he thanked me for the tip.

Now that Ted and I are finally done with the Washington business and are on our way home in our nice blue plane and I have an idea.

"Hey Ted, let's stop in KC and see everyone before I go home."

"OK. I know Mike will be very glad to see you." He said. "He always says that he wishes that you would include him in some of your cases."

I'm beginning to enjoy riding in the plane more than being the pilot.

I was chuckling about Ted's remarks. Wait till he sees what's coming tonight.

I thought I would want to be in the driver's seat, But I'm giving that up if Ted continues to enjoy it as much as he does.

Once we landed and put the plane away, we had to find Ted's car. It's always hard to find. It's that big white '55 Cadillac that you could see from space. He left his car in the extended time lot. It was a brisk walk and we were on our way. Soon we were pulling up in front of the Family Restaurant in Platte City. I wonder how many times I have done this.

We walked in and Sally yelled when she saw us.

"Mike! Mike! Come out here!" She yelled.

Mike ran out of the kitchen and right into me.

"Hello cousin. You were wonderful! I haven't seen acting like that in years! Did you read all the news stories about you?'

"Wait a minute! Mike? That was you? The crazy guy calling himself Little Big Town?" Ted said. The look of shock on Ted's face was funny in itself.

"Yes! I'm famous, but no one will ever know. Did you contact the real LBT?" Mike said.

"Wait a minute! How did you get out of the asylum. No! How did you know to be there? No! Why didn't I know anything about this? NO! "What about the press pass that said Little Big Town?

"You do know that we have an ID card machine, don't you?" Mike said. "I made one special."

"The guard took me in and they graciously showed me to a room. We know how these places work, so we worked them. DJ made a special mask for me. I was wearing special reversible clothes. I took the disguise off and I shined my shoes while I was in the room."

"I saved the mask and wig and stuffed them in the envelope addressed to DJ laying on the table. Then I dropped them in the mail box on the way out. I wanted to leave the crummy hat and tie in the room, but I didn't want any evidence left behind. So they are in the closet in my room here."

"The guard was waiting in the car and he took me to the airport, where I had a ticket for KC in the name of DJ. I walked into the airport terminal, got in line and boarded the plane like a normal tourist would do. No problem, here I am."

"But, what about your hair? You're bald!" Ted said.

"I didn't want any clues to be dropped around, so I shaved. What if someone saw two different colors of hair on the LBT guy when he was in the press room?" Mike said. "Besides, I had a hat with the name of a New York team there. It had tape on the inside so it would stick to me as I walked out."

"Ted, we didn't want to involve you in a crazy under thought out plan that might go wrong and cause us all a lot of trouble." Mike said.

"But! Oh well. OK. I think I understand." Ted said.

"I can't remember the last time I have had so much fun! I'd like to do this again!" Mike said.

"Did you get to talk the the quartet yet?" Ted asked.

"Yes. They all had a huge laugh that some idiot reporter didn't know who they were and would write such a vicious story about them. But the best laugh was that Mike could be four people at once and no one could see through it."

"I'll bet they won't forget Little Big Town again." Mike said.

"Why did you pick Little Big Town for the name?" Ted said.

"Easy!   There are three names, none of which could be a man's name.   They are a quartet.   Self explanatory.   There are two beautiful girls.   Again Self explanatory.   They are a famous country music group and everyone should know that.   Except that idiot in DC."   Mike said.

"I hope we get to see Little Big Town some time at a concert or something."   Mike said.

"Stranger things have happened."

"I've got to get back home.   I have work to do.   Norm needs me.   He can't continue his work without me bothering him every few days."

Chapter 9

Those Doctors

I wanted to have a big party after we got home and I was hoping that the big deal room addition would be done by then. Well, most of it was.

There are a lot of little finishing touches that need finished. But that won't stop me from enjoying all the fancy food that the people I work with will be glad to bring to a cookout.

I called ahead and told Lopez my idea and the next day they were all coming in the back way and oooing and aahing at the room and the patio that dominated the whole yard.

Denise and the women began bringing pans and bowls of food out and filling the three tables that we had there. All the women made a lot of sounds about the outdoor kitchen. Denise had filled the fridge with pop and ice.

Norm and Lopez came over and sat down with me at one of small tables. We watched and talked about nothing in particular.

I don't get to sit down and just talk with Norm very often. We seem to be much more involved in getting cars and trucks for people. It is one of the joys in my life.

"Hey DJ, you never have told me why the drugs thing is so important to you." Norm said.

"I know that I talk about drugs a lot. I have always said that drugs will screw up your life. And they will! The drugs that I have always talked about have been illegal, off-the-street drugs."

"But to make a comparison for you with the legal, life saving drugs that the doctors prescribe, I have a little true story for you."

I decided to tell Norm the whole story.

"This all happened some time around Thanksgiving of a year in the past."

"As I said, this is a true story. I have added some cruel and unusual punishment into it just for fun. Names are being withheld to protect the guilty.

"We had been living and working in Wichita for a few years before all this happened. Sometime around Thanksgiving, I noticed a red and pink bump in the middle of my forehead which had not been there the last time I shaved.

"I felt it and examined it as closely as I could, but I'm no doctor, and I didn't know what I was looking for. It looked like a bee sting, a pimple, a cyst or something like that.

"I watched it every day for a couple of weeks. Every day it looked a little different. During those next few days, I watched the bump closely. I noticed it had changed color. Last week it was pink and red, but today it was red and purple. But that could just be because of the color or the amount of blood inside.

"Then it changed shape. At first it was round like a pimple, but today it was a little longer that it was wide. I noticed what looked like a corner, but there's no corners in round things.

"Then it seemed to move slightly. Not that I could see, but that I could remember. Later that day I called from our office and made an appointment with Dr. Anderson for a couple of days later and forgot about it.

"None of this was good news. I had read about this kind of thing and the answer was always the same thing, "it's cancer".

"I had known Dr. Anderson for several years by now. We raced together in road rallies and went to car shows together.

I drive a Porsche automobile and I have gone to the races, auto crosses and rallies for years. He has a Corvette. I have known Doc Anderson for several years because of the racing and because he is ethical and true. It's a good thing to hear the truth when you visit your doctor.

"I called the Doc's office and made an appointment. When I reported to Dr. Anderson's office, he examined it and said, "Uh, oh.""

"I'm an engineer and never studied medicine or anything relating to it, except nurses when I was young."

"Now I don't know about you, but if you go to the doctor and he examines you and then he says, "Uh, oh", I know what that means. It means that you sit down, grab your knees, bend over and kiss your SELF goodbye."

"I want you to go see Dr. Smith today. He will be able to tell us exactly what we have here." He said. I don't remember his name, so Dr. Smith will do.

"Doctor Anderson sent me to a dermatologist that same day. He had called ahead and the other doctor got me in without waiting. That's a clue that something bad is going on, too."

"I went to Dr. Smith a dermatologist. I had heard of a skin cancer called Basic Cell something, maybe that's what this was."

"I walked into his office and handed a slip of paper to the receptionist and she ran back to a room and passed the paper through the door."

"Then she came out and took me to room three and told me that the doc would be right in to see me."

"The visit to the dermatologist was the same as the one with Dr. Anderson."

"Dr. Smith came in with three young guys dressed in those starched white jackets that look like they should be in a cartoon, to look at and touch my pretty little spot on my forehead. I can see more "Uh, oh's" coming."

"Doctor Smith looked at my forehead and reached up and felt it. "Uh oh.""

"The three interns all did the same thing again and I got three more "Uh oh's". Five 'uh oh's' in one day. I thought this was bad, but now it's catastrophic!"

"This isn't so bad. We should be OK with this. We'll be fixing it all real soon." He said.

"Don't you just love it when they say 'we', when all the time it's really 'you'?"

"Doctor Smith had the nurse give me a shot of Novocain in my forehead. What fun this is today. It felt like she was driving a sword through my head. I expected blood to come running down the back of my neck. She brought what looked like a hammer and chisel with her. Wow! Maybe this is the way they remove this stuff from your forehead."

"He took the tools from her and after a few minutes he hit the punch in the middle of my forehead. He did what he called a 'punch biopsy' on the bump. My blood squirted on the doc and me. He casually put a band aid on it and said, "You'll need to go to the lab for blood and urine. She'll show you where to go."

"When you're done at the lab, go home, I'll call you as soon as I get the biopsy." He said.

"The lab was down the hall and around the corner. This is turning out to be so much fun. At least I didn't have one of those gowns with no back in it as I ran around their hospital."

"Giving blood is said to be voluntary. They take lots of blood from lots of people. I have a good friend who is a nurse and she has assured me that the doctors are not vampires. But what do they do with all that blood that they take from us. Maybe a shot of whiskey would make a real Bloody Mary."

"It was the next day that Dr. Smith called me and wanted me to come to his office. They always want you to come to their office when the news is bad. And this was, I knew it."

"What is it, Leprosy?" I asked,

"Oh, no, it's not that bad, it's only Lymphoma."
Dr. Smith said.

"ONLY Lymphoma? Are you kidding? Lymphoma and Only do not go together in the same sentence! Ever! Everything with an oma on the end is cancer and cancer is fatal. Oklahoma is the only one I know that is not cancer.' I paused while I tried to take in all he said. "At least with Leprosy, I will continue to live, but I'll just be scratching all the time. But, with Only Lymphoma, I get to take a dirt nap."

"But we caught it early". He said.

"Like that makes a difference. Oh goodie, we caught it early. Everybody knows that Lymphoma is fatal. So catching it early means that you don't die this week. It'll be a few more weeks, but you still gonna die."

"With Leprosy, I could still live and scratch all day."

"Its Lymphoma, but it's OK. This is the only one that's not fatal. It's DHL." He said.

"I'll bet that stands for you are Dead Here Lymphoma."

"It's Lymphoma. But it's not that bad." He said.

"How not bad could it be if it's Lymphoma?

"You all know how they lie."

"You go to the doc and say, "My left arm has been hurting for a while."

"So, he looks at it and feels it and says, "It's not so bad. It's Only Lymphoma. There's that name again. Go home and call me in two weeks, and we'll look at it again."

"Three days later, your arm falls off."

"I didn't know what that DHL thing meant, but I had always heard that Lymphoma was fatal. So I told my wife and the family and we all prepared for the end of the story."

"The horn on my head grew daily until it looked like a purple plum was stuck to my forehead. I look like a unicorn with a purple horn."

"I went to the hospital for radiation, and the purple plum melted down until it was flat. I was amazed at how it just shriveled up. You have to go to the hospital because that's where the radiator is."

"I thought I was done with the Oma problem, but big surprise, look what comes next."

"The next part was the worst. Chemo. They gave me chemo called CHOP. Those are the initials for the drugs. The last part of the word on each was toxin, or something like that. I had C toxin, H toxin O toxin and Prednisone. We all know what 'toxin' means, it's a fancy word for poison."

"I'd have been better off if they just chopped my head off and been done with it."

"I swelled up like the Pillsbury Dough Boy. I put on 60 pounds in less than six months. We lived in Colorado before we moved to Wichita and I wore cowboy boots and a hat and rode horses all the time."

"My feet swelled up from a size eleven to a size twenty or thirty, and now I had to cut a really good pair of boots off my feet with a pair of shears so I could walk. That's how fast the stuff was working."

"The chemo was injected into the back of my left hand near the little finger. And it was so strong that it burnt the inside of the veins that run through the wrist toward the arm. The hand swelled up and turned purple and the pain was excruciating for the duration until the next meeting. When I get to do it all over again."

"When I told the oncologist about it, he suggested that he put in a port through my chest directly into my heart, so my hand wouldn't hurt. I didn't think that this was a good idea since the toxin would burn the heart and I would be back to square one, dirt nap."

"I would take it on Tuesday, race home get undressed and spend the next two or three days in the bathroom throwing up all the wonderful stuff they gave me. Then there was a brief period where I thought I was going to live but wished I would die. I would partially recuperate the third week, go to work for a few days and then start the whole cycle over again."

"I did this for six courses. All my hair fell out during the second and third dose of the magic elixir. The hair in my ears and nose, the hair on my arms and legs and all the dark brown hair on my head. I didn't know it, but the hair would change color when it did finally come back in. It's a little lighter in color now. At least I didn't have to shave for those months. By the time it was done I was worn out, physically, mentally, emotionally and I said to God. "I'm ready Lord, take me now."

"His reply was this. "See me later.""

"And here I am, doing what I can. Still writing. Still talking. Still breathing. Thanks to God."

"There are a few things that I learned from all this pain and panic. Maybe you have to go through some pain to learn something. Maybe doctors aren't really vampires, but that hasn't been completely proven yet."

"Maybe they don't lie all the time. Just sometimes when you might feel bad or pain about the truth."

"They make way too much money. Everybody knows that. But they seem to be able to make us well again when we go to see them."

"I suppose that's something."

Norm thanked me for the long sad story of cancer and all the pain and suffering.

"I had no idea that you went through all that with chemo. People seem to make light of it and blow it off as if it didn't count." Norm said.

"I have one funny one for you now Norm."

I suppose you know the pharmaceutical companies are always looking for a new and better drug to cure something.

We already know that the drugs are identified by the first letter of their name.

Onc of the new chemists at a pharmaceutical company found that 'A' did something that he wanted to do. But it wasn't strong enough. So he went through twenty five or thirty letters to find something hat would match with A and would still do the job. It was Z. But Z wasn't strong enough so he added another Z to the mix. Now it was strong enough but it wouldn't run. So he added some R. Now it was running but it was going too fast, so he added something from gentle. He added a little T to tone it down.

This chemist had an eye to the future and he decided to make a little more. Once it was all concocted he needed to bake it over night to get the right consistency.

But as always, there is something that gets in the middle of everything and fouls it up. And it happened when the chemist opened the oven to inspect his formula.

It came out looking like this.

RAZZ AMA TAZZ.

They are sure that this will cure everything there is, no matter what. But, with the AMA in the middle of things, there will always be something wrong.

Chapter 10

Arizona

We've been to DC before and this time was no different. There's always someone who wants a sound bite on camera from someone they don't recognize, and when they get it back to their office, someone will say, "Who's that? That's nobody!" and then throw it away.

I just don't give them a chance to see me and stick a camera and mic in my face. My disguises make all the difference for me.

It was a long and strange few days in the eastern part of the country. Now that we are back, there are a lot of those little things that I have to do just to catch up. First is Denise and the kids, a couple of nice home cooked meals and a night's sleep in my own bed. Second is some play time and fun with the girls and Harry and Bruce.

Then I have to call Earl. He might have some work that I can help him with. And of course, a stop at the shop to see Norm is always in order.

As usual Norm was busy with three jobs at once and he didn't see us walk in. I wonder what rare or classic car he is hiding today. I wonder what rare or classic car Earl would fall in love with.

I carefully strained to uncover a hidden gem. I peeked under all the car covers I could, I craned my head to look in back of every car I could find, nothing. This isn't like him.

Them I saw something out of place. A car was sandwiched in between four others. It was blue, low, with a cover only on the front end. It is a Porsche!

But it was wrecked. The more I looked at it, the worse it got. It would need all the sheet metal straightened or replaced. There's no telling what the motor and transaxle is like. I pulled the cover back in place and gave up.

Then I saw Norm coming out of the office.

"OK! Where is it?"

"What?" He has his innocent face on now.

"The car you are hiding, of course."

"Me?" He said. "I would never hide anything from you, DJ!" More innocence.

"OK. But I wanted to suggest we get something special for Earl. I don't have a clue what he likes. Did you get any ideas from talking to him?"

"Actually I did. But vague. I think he would like a truck of some kind. Maybe a pickup, but maybe not." He said. "You know that I frequent all the used car lots and scrap yards in the area, don't you?"

"I know the guy that owns that scrap yard out in Ellicott. Well he has two 1949 or 50 Studebaker pickups there. I looked at them last week and made a deal for them. He will deliver them as soon as he can." Norm said.

"Those have to be the ugliest pickups in history."

"Maybe, but I'd bet he will love it." Norm said. "Besides, I will have two of every part in them."

There are a lot of small churches in the small towns around the Springs. To name a few, Payton, Simla, Falcon, Limon, Calhan, Ellicot, Yoder, Rush, Fountain, Manitou and Pueblo. We have done a few houses, but they never have covering over the windows. Sometimes there are storm windows over them.

We have a lot of Colleges locally as well as Military bases, like the USAF Academy, Fort Carson, the Olympic Center and Ent AF Base. We don't get many calls for stained glass from any of them.

I called Earl as soon as I left Norm's place to see if he needed some help. Earl said he got a call from a church in Pueblo while I was out of town. They got hit with a big windstorm and several of the windows were broken.

He had already done the initial inspection and negotiations. But there was one sticking point. The large round window in the highest peak of the building was broken and letting the weather in on the seats below.

Earl and I drove down to see it. He climbed up to the top from the inside and measured everything, but we couldn't take the window out or put the new window in from the inside. He had a piece of foam board in his truck and we cut it to go in the hole and left it. At least it will keep out the rain.

There must be a way to do this, but we'll need to think hard about this one. We'll come back later.

Lopez and I have been to three of the states called the 'Four Corners' now. Colorado, Utah and New Mexico have all been visited by our intrepid crews and we have found a few terrorists hiding in the bushes. Now it's time to visit the last of the four, Arizona.

As usual Lopez asked for volunteers to go to Arizona and spend a couple weeks in the heat looking for the bad guys. And as usual all hands went up when he asked. Boy, I really like this group of officers.

Arizona is a big state and we will need more than two teams for this one. One team will take Interstate Forty, one will take I-10, one will take the north-south route of I-17 and I-19 and one to take I-8.

Lopez picked four team leaders and wrote the locations on pieces of paper and had them draw one from his hat. There are several big towns and lots of impressionable kids available for the bad guys to influence. I hope we can stop them all.

I drew the north-south route, so we started in Nogales and spent three days in Tuscon. Then off the main road to Oro Valley, Florence and Apache Junction. I especially wanted to see Apache Junction, since I knew a little about this town from friends.

We spent a couple of hours driving and walking around the town. I didn't see anything especially interesting or unusual about the place. So we were on our way. I had to laugh when I saw one white kid with blonde hair on the street. Not too many of them around here. Then Mesa and around Phoenix on the way to Flagstaff.

By that time, my guys were worn out so we took in a dinner theater and an early night in bed. By morning I had eight hours of sleep and was feeling like a new man. Now a long drive up to Page with a few side trips along the way. Now all we have to do is find our way home. I didn't get to see Davis Monthan Air Force Base, but I've been there before.

After we found our hometown and had a night's sleep, we all returned to work the next day and we compared notes. We didn't do as well as I expected. Maybe the bad guys don't like the extreme heat and sand. But we did catch a few fish and reeled them in to our friends at the FBI. I love them guys.

Once we got settled later in the week, Earl and I took a trip to that church in Pueblo with the round window we don't know what to do with. There is some construction going on in this part of the town, and I was standing there with Earl when the foreman asked what we were doing.

"A round lexan window needs to be put over that round window way up in the peak there." Earl said as he pointed at the window.

After Earl explained it to him, the foreman came up with a solution.

"See that guy over there? He could raise you two up to that window." the foreman said.

"How?"

"There is an excavator right over there." He said pointing toward a large yellow machine with a huge bucket and a really big arm. You could stand in the bucket with your tools and be right in front of the window."

I don't believe it! Of course Earl picked the most dangerous way to do the job. Earl looked it over and the three of us talked about this suggestion. I would have bet that Earl would not have wanted to do this - - - But.

"Sure!" Earl said. "Let's go!"

I thought I was crazy, but Earl takes the cake! So we got our tools and the lexan and climbed into the bucket of this big machine and away we went, up, up and away to the window four stories above the ground.

I fed Earl the tools and he had the broken window out in fifteen minutes. The last time we were here he climbed up inside the building and measured the lexan to fit outside the window. Then in his shop last week he cut it to fit and had it all ready. It only took us a few more minutes to have it installed also and we were on the ground again.

"That was kind of fun! We should do that more often." He said and laughed. Then we all laughed.

I can't believe this guy.

Lopez and I have been planning several weeks ahead on every idea that we have. We are trying to stay ahead of the bad guys. In between, we help Earl, help Norm and anyone else that needs it. Earl called me a few days later and said that he had a short ten minute job that he needed my help with,

Of course, I said OK.

We drove to a little town east of the Springs called Calhan. I've been there a lot because that's where the El Paso County fair is held every year. He got a call from someone in Calhan about glass. So here we go out Highway 24 east to Calhan.

The guy that called us works at the lumber yard there. Buddy does all the maintenance for most of the people around that area. One of the churches there had a bird fly onto a window high in their spire. Must have been a big bird.

"Not another one of those!" I said as I craned my neck to see up to the window.

Buddy has a scaffold installed and bolted into his pickup bed. He uses it a lot for the roof work and high reach places he needs to get to for the work he does out there.

Buddy backed the pickup up to the building, shut down the engine put it in gear and pulled the emergency brake. Earl crawled up to the pickup bed. Then up to the scaffold, and with me holding the ladder, he climbed the ladder to reach the broken glass window.

This area where we live is called the high plains. It is well known for the winds here, sometimes high winds. We don't get tornadoes, or hurricanes or big thunderstorms. But we do get high winds from time to time.

When Earl was on the scaffold, a big gust of wind suddenly moved the truck a few inches to one side and back and Earl fell off. More like he sailed off and fortunately landed in the bushes around the property. I almost went with him, but I was holding tightly.

Buddy has taken care of this church for years and had planted some very special soft bushes all around. Earl landed in the middle of one patch of them, feet first.

Then Earl jumped up with his arms in the air like he was signaling a touchdown and said, "I'm OK!"

He must be part cat. But now he has sore feet and legs. I hope that's all there is.

It's a good thing we have help here. Buddy carried a piece of the plastic foam and climbed the ladder and filled the hole until we can return and do it right.

With Earl flying around and jumping twelve to fifteen feet off of a ladder, it's time to return to the city and, I hope, normal.

"Thanks Buddy. We'll be back to finish the job when Superman comes back down to earth. See ya."

Earl was a little shook so I drove back to town. I dropped Earl and his van off at his house and drove to Casey's for a nice big sandwich for Denise and me.

I have known a funny girl named Bertha a long time, we always make each other laugh. But this time there was no laughing. She gave me a tip she got from her girlfriend, Maryanne, back east. You gotta believe a girl named Bertha. She has always been straight with me.

"Maryanne and I was talking when she mentioned that she saw some guys loading big packages into a truck at the airport." She said.

"What's so unusual about that?"

"She said they were really big. Too big for one guy to carry by himself. And I've heard you mention this town's name before." She said.

"What town is that?"

"She lives in Danbury, Connecticut." She said.

Boy! What a shock! That surprised me! I immediately called Lopez and told him what she said.

"It looks like we have a trip scheduled to Danbury soon. Aren't you packed yet?" Lopez said.

We took four of our people and booked a flight out of Peterson to Hartford. I called Martin our friendly FBI guy and told him everything.

"I hope this is the one. We've been trying to close this down for years now." He said. "I'll meet you there."

It's only a sixty mile drive from Hartford to Danbury. I had called ahead and rented two cars, I got two of our people and Lopez got Martin and the rest. We made good time because of the Interstate Route.

We drove directly to the airport and parked near the office.

Chapter 11

Where is Danbury?

Martin made sure we had the search warrants in hand when we arrived at the airport. We were careful when we entered the office. You never know what might be waiting for you.

When I walked into the office, it was empty. How strange. The rest of the facility seemed to be humming along. I wanted to interrogate some one, but no one volunteered. All of us searched the whole building. Everyone was walking and feeling the walls for hidden doors and latches. Finally one of the officers found a locked nondescript door in an out of the way place.

"That has to be it!" Said Martin.

One of the officers stepped up to pick the lock and enter the door. I followed that officer and another down a stairway to the basement, where we found a big empty room with a printing press located in the center section.

There are shelves on all sides around it. But the room was completely bare. It looked like it had been swept and mopped. There was not even dust on the shelves.

"Well, there's nothing else to do but question everyone here. Workers, owners, passengers, everyone. Let's get started." Martin said.

He and Lopez began rounding them up and filled the office with people. We had a mass question and answer game for a few minutes until we singled out a few who seemed to know something from the ones who obviously didn't have a clue.

I took names, addresses, phone numbers and photos of everyone and sent the people home. Then I sent all the photos to Jerry Vernon for a quick look. Our officers checked them all for weapons and other items. We found some paperwork in one desk. It looked like they had been warned that we were on our way and they cleared out very fast.

I thought we had that problem fixed. This probably means that we will be forced to go to DC again! Damn!

I pulled everything out of the desk drawer and piled it on top. One of the girls who had been held there saw a photo and picked it up and said, "Hey, I know him!"

That got my attention!

"Do you know this guy?"

"Yeah! I think he's a teacher someplace around here, but I can't remember where." She said.

I hope I can trigger her memory.

As we went one by one through the people we had in the office, we found one with a wrong ID. It had his name, address, and a photo of someone else.

"You are John Russell?"

"Yes, sir." He said.

"Why is the photo here not a photo of you?"

"There was a lot of people getting their license and it must have been picked up wrong." He said.

"Where were you born?"

"Danbury, Connecticut." He said proudly.

"Do you know where we are right now?"

"No." He said.

When I questioned him, he said that he was born in Danbury. Not that he was born here.

It looks like the terrorists don't even know where they are or what or where Danbury is. I motioned to Martin and he gladly put the handcuffs on him.

We have let most of the people go home and as I was wandering around the hangar, feeling forlorn and dejected, I spotted a scrap of paper on the floor. I picked it up and there was some scribbling on it. I couldn't make it out.

"Ann, could you look at this for me?"

I like to have Ann Webster with me on one of these crazy trips. She is so smart it's scary. I would bet that her IQ is as high or higher than Ted's. And that's saying a lot.

I handed her the paper and she smiled a big one.

"It says here that a Congressman has been seen here nearly every day for the past several months. The writer believes he is in charge of something here. There have been many foreign looking people, mostly men, coming and going. There has also a lot of cargo hauled in and out of here." She said.

"I wonder how the writer knew the person they saw was a Congressman."

Ann and I talked to the girl who said she recognized the man in the photo. She said that she was sure he is a teacher in a school somewhere around there.

"If I knew which school, I could pose as a visiting professor and maybe I'd get lucky."

"I could go to the school board with a story of some kind and find out who and where he is." Ann said.

"It's the last week of the semester and I could go to other classes and look for terrorists, teachers or students and get names, photos, any other information."

"Great idea, we'll go together." She said.

Ann and I went to the City Hall and the hospital to find birth certificates and drivers licenses on the suspicious ones. We asked questions and showed photos of the ones we found. When we were at the DMV, one of the clerks there told us that she recognized one of them. I didn't see this one coming at all.

"Why yes, I know this man. That's George Jones. He lives over on Sapphire Street." She said.

George Jones! I have heard that name before. I called Jerry Vernon in DC and asked him to show this photo around and tell me if he was one of the George Jones' that we picked up. I hope.

No luck. I thought it was too good to be true.

"But wait a minute, DJ! The other photo is a Congressman from up there." Jerry said.

"Now we're getting somewhere! Are you sure? Can you get me some good information on him?"

"Sure. I have all that right here. His name is Clayton. I'll send you his photo and resume." Jerry said.

Ann, Lopez and I got our heads together outside where no one could hear us.

"OK! We have a George Jones and a Congressman, named Clayton, working together. We know there is counterfeit printing going on somewhere. Maybe George Jones is a teacher at some school near here. We have five George Jones' in custody. What do we do now?"

"We have six George Jones'. Lopez said. "That one at Belle View!"

"No. That was Mike."

"What?" He said.

I stood there laughing. Neither one of them knew.

"I'll tell you later. I'm going with Ann and pose as a visiting professor from Utah. That should get me into the inside of some of the schools and maybe we'll learn something. But first I must call the Director and make sure he knows about the leak."

The secretary answered the phone. "Hello." She said.

"Hello. This is DJ. Could I speak with the Director. I have some very important news for him."

There was a short pause while she told him who was on the phone.

"DJ! What can I do for you?" He said.

"Sir I wanted you to know we found another leak in our service."

I told him how we found the airport building and how everything had been cleaned up before we arrived. I know it had to be because someone warned the people here that we were coming.

I also explained about George Jones, the Congressman and the printing press. I sent him photos of both of them.

"These two are terrorists and probably counter-feiters and we need to arrest and confine them both."

Ann and I spent the next two days going from school to school and questioning them and showing the photos. We got some maybes and some 'I don't knows', but no 'yeses'.

Finally, one of the teachers showed us an annual from their school and there was a photo of our man.

"That's Frank Emerson! He teaches Social Studies." She said. "He has been here in this high school for several years."

Of course! So George Jones is Frank Emerson. That's probably a fake name too. What else would a terrorist teacher teach but Social Studies. They are trying to destroy our social network. Now all we need to do is find him and his accomplice, the Congressman.

Lopez had a good idea. "Why don't we have a broken window where we could put a man lift or some scaffolds there in the airport, and we could look in the windows for the bad guys as we pretend to work." He said.

"Sounds good to me, but who is is going to spend their whole day up on the scaffolds?"

Lopez immediately went to the office and began writing a schedule. He asked each of our people which times they could take the watch. Soon he had a full day worked out.

I called Jerry again. I'm in a hurry to get something started here.

I never paid much attention to the governing part of the Government in DC, but now I am saddled with a problem with a counterfeiter there. The worst part is that none of us knows anything . I have called Jerry and the Speaker for help, but they don't know anything yet either.

Jerry found the names of all the aides and the secretary, but we can't find the people. We had been discussing the problem when we were told by one of the teachers about a superintendent who dragged a teacher out of the school by her hair with the help from a security guard.

We were told it was because he didn't like what she said. This was too good to be true. We checked her out. We interviewed the guard, and he told us an amazing story about the superintendent. We talked to teachers and students and were astonished at what we heard.

The crazy superintendent was on the wrong side of everything he said.

I made a special trip to see the school board and told them all I knew about him. I had to show them my badge and gun and explain what we were doing before they paid much attention.

"You have only a few choices. If you keep him in the school system, I will think you are working with him. If you remove him I will arrest him and charge him with assault and he will be in jail before the sun goes down."

They removed him and charges were filed against him. I made it a point to personally put the cuffs on him and turn him over to our FBI friends. I liked it. I would like to remove all the off-center teachers and admin people in our schools. We don't need terrorism being taught to kids so young that they can't distinguish good from bad.

"Congressman Clayton has been missing since last week. He told someone that he would be out with his constituency. I think that's a distraction. He did not make the last vote. He must not be the leak. He must be the one they warned. That means the leak is in the SS or the FBI. I don't like either of those conclusions." Jerry said.

"Is there any way that someone else knew we were going to Danbury besides us and Martin's people?"

"Let me work on that. I hope you have a good idea." Jerry said. "I'll call all of his aides and other helpers. I think we can find him."

"I have another idea. Could we get some kind of info on birth certificates of who was actually born here and have a list to eliminate the good ones? So far, if anyone says Danbury, we arrest them, but there are some good ones."

I'm sure Jerry will work on the problem and get us some info very soon.

After we left the airport, we scouted Clayton's district . No one had seen him. We went to his office, Martin had the Police open the office for us, but there was no one there. It was the same as at the airport. Cleaned out and swept clean. Why would they sweep it?

Martin called in the fingerprinting guys to do the airport. The fingerprinting continued to his office. He asked them to be on call. We are going to each aides home now.

Jerry gave me all the names and addresses of his private secretary and all of the aides. We spent a lot of time finding all the addresses. We found all the houses empty, but there was still furniture and food and other things in the houses. It looked like they had just walked out and took a trip to some relatives houses.

The secretary's house was not swept clean, it just looked like she went to the store and didn't come back. The two aides live together when they are in Wash DC, but separate in Danbury. Everything in Danbury was empty and clean.

Martin called for some help with any relatives of Clayton or any of his staff.

Martin and Lopez decided that we could wait out the results of our questions at home. I agree! We all drove to Hartford and returned the cars and took the next flight to get home.

I know we'll have to go back there again.

My first stop when I return to the Springs is always Denise. After we do a little hugging and kissing, we talk about what I've done and what has been going here at home.

"The room is done and the outside kitchen is done too. I am so happy about what we have in the back yard now. The room is as big as the front room, and with more windows. The windows are bigger too. I have light from every direction and I can see the mountains now." She said.

"Have you tried the outdoor kitchen yet?"

"Yes, and the girls and I love it. We had dinner out here the first day after Jason finished it, and he brought his wife over too. We all had a great time. You're going to love it." She said.

The first day we got back I got together with Lopez and Norm. We talked about a party at Norm's place and the reason for it.

"When Earl was here he said that he would like to have a really old pickup truck. I found two ugly 1949 Studebakers in that place in Ellicott. I bought them and we finished one using all the parts from both." Norm said.

"What do you mean 'ugly' Norm?" Lopez asked.

"Take a look." Norm took us over to the car cover in the back of the shop and pulled it off to the floor.

It looked like a man's face with a scowl on it. The headlights are the eyes, the fenders the cheeks, and the grille his mouth, turned down in the corners.

"Wow! I have never seen one of these before! You're right! It's not the prettiest pickup Is ever seen, but it looks brand new." Lopez said.

"It might as well be brand new, we went through every part, cleaned and restored it all. Except for the year on the thing, it's brand new now." Norm said.

"Tell everyone, we'll take off early. They should bring food, music, their wives and kids and anything else they want. Let's have some fun."

The day of the party came and I had to make some excuse to get Earl to come to Norm's shop with me. I deliberately made sure that Earl and I were a few minutes late. I wanted everyone to be there when I brought him in.

As we were driving there I was explaining the Foundation and it's mission to him. He said that there were a few people in his church who could use our kind of help.

"I have some applications there in the glove box. Why don't you take a few and hand them out and explain it to them. We will be glad to help them out. Besides, we have more money than we need anyway."

We both laughed at that one for the rest of the drive.

When we walked into Norm's shop everyone was going through the line to get food and sitting around talking.

"Good afternoon everyone. I brought a very special friend with me today. This is Earl Cohen. He is the one who does the stained glass that I've told you about."

"Earl doesn't know it, but Norm and I have a little surprise for him. There in the middle of the shop is an old rag covering something. This will be a shock to you as well as to Earl, so cover your eyes and we'll unveil it."

Lopez and I took Earl to the car cover and as he stood there, we pulled the cover off onto the floor.

Everyone went 'Oohhh' when they saw it. Several of them said, "What is that?" Earl stared at it and smiled a big smile.

"Did you make that for me?" He asked.

"Yes we did." Norm said.

"What is it? I've never seen anything like this before." Earl said.

"This is a fully restored and completely road ready 1949 Studebaker Pickup. It has been inspected and licensed and is ready to drive anywhere. Here are the keys and the registration."

I handed him the keys and everyone applauded. He stood there and was embarrassed, but smiling the whole time.

Chapter 12

Who Is A Terrorist?

As soon as we got back from our favorite city in Connecticut, Lopez and I planned a conference with the whole force to try to get some ideas about what to do and how to handle this problem.

He decided to have the meeting in the conference room. We moved all the extra chairs from the offices and tried to make it comfortable. We need help, and I don't want anyone hurting more than me.

I was elected by Lopez to explain everything.

It's easier for me to move around when I talk to a group this size. So I stood up and walked around the front of the room as I talked about all the information we have.

"I did a little research on the Senate and House. Let me read you a few notes that might help us. I have a notebook full of notes and facts relating to everything we have found."

"Representatives receive allowances to hire an office staff of about three or four. There is always a secretary and there could be administrative assistants."

"There is an allowance for one round trip to their home district each session."

"This Congressman's office is located in the House Office Building. Lobbyists are always trying to influence the Congress and their people to vote for their pet projects. In order to influence the legislators, they try to have frequent contacts with Congressmen. The lobbyists always want these contacts to look accidental, but they are not. They are well thought out."

"They try to persuade the Congress to favor their group. Sometimes a lobbyist will try to influence Congressmen with favors or money. This is called bribery and it is illegal. But that has never stopped it from happening."

"Some lobbying is the best way citizens can make their wishes known. Public meetings in churches, schools and auditoriums called 'Town Hall Meetings' seem to be the best."

"Lobbyists are required to register and submit quarterly reports along with the bills they are interested in to Congress."

"OK. Let's take this in steps."

"Assume Congressman Clayton is a terrorist. How was he notified? By whom? Where did he go? When? How did he get there? Where are his people?"

"Next, assume Clayton is not a terrorist. Why did he get notified? Was someone else the one who was notified? If that's true, then Clayton must be the counterfeiter. Who was the one who notified him? Where are the others?"

"Next assume one of his people is the terrorist. Why wouldn't Clayton notice? How did someone else know he was at the airport?"

"Now assume Emerson is the terrorist. Why wouldn't Clayton notice? How did someone else know he was at the airport? Check phone records. What if it's a cell phone? We know that Emerson is a terrorist, because he used the George Jones thing and he knows about Danbury."

"Then assume Emerson is not a terrorist. Can't."

"How did all that ink and paper get moved out of the basement? We know there is a dock in the back. But everything is heavy. Too heavy to move by hand. Anyone would have needed a forklift and a truck. None around there. No one saw the vehicles or equipment we just mentioned. Everyone would see the action. Either they are all involved or were not there when it happened."

"If Clayton and Emerson are both terrorists they might kidnap or kill the others, or any others that are working with him."

"Emerson must know about the printing press, that makes him a counterfeiter too."

"I wonder who the guys were who carried out the big packages that people saw? What was in the packages? Money? Counterfeit?"

"One last item. Our friends in the FBI got a genealogy company to test Clayton's DNA. They found that he is a cousin to that professor at Boulder. Remember him? His name was Finch, and he let three of the worst fiends into this country. The Congressman named Wilson was one of them."

"Did I miss anything?"

There was a slight pause as everyone thought about what I said after I finished.

"We have had some ideas that these guys might be psychopaths trying to do some evil work. Do you think this might be part of it?" John asked.

"I have a good friend here in town who is a certified genius in this field. I went to him some time ago and asked about this very subject. He told me to study a certain book that he gave me for a few weeks."

"In it I found what was called the Psychopathy checklist. I listed the ones that might pertain. There are nine categories that will be pretty obvious. Let me read them to you, Get your pencils."

"Glibness, a grandiose sense of self-worth, pathological lying, manipulation, lack of remorse, guilt or empathy, impulsiveness, irresponsibility, and failure to accept responsibility."

"The big thing about this stuff is that it is subjective. One person might say that the suspect is manipulative and none of the others apply. That doesn't score high."

"You would need to have several of these items show up in a person to start you on their track."

"Then there are some that you couldn't know about unless you had an actual meeting with the person. I won't go into them now but there are eleven of them."

"What I am saying is that we shouldn't jump to any conclusions until we have a medical degree in psychology."

"For us as law enforcement personnel, we should use them to eliminate the ones that don't fit and narrow the suspect list."

"We do know that these terrorists hate Christians! We know that for sure. Let me give you something to ponder."

"The United States of America was founded by a small group of people fleeing from the religious oppression of England in the 1600's."

"These people were Christians and they founded a Christian Nation. The Christian name hearkens back to Jesus the Christ. The sequence of the numbering of the years we live by starts with Jesus. Consequently this country also reaches back to Israel since Jesus was a Jew."

"Nowhere in all the words that have been written or spoken over the many years of existence of this country has the word Muslim ever been spoken about the foundation of this country. The United States is not now, nor ever will be, a Muslim nation."

"The liberal press and all the misguided principals and teachers in all the schools across this country would do well in reining in their ranting about wanting this country to be a Muslim country."

"It's long past time for an overhaul in the teaching profession and their prejudiced unions. I look forward to seeing some of these super-prejudiced school superintendents go out of school in handcuffs."

"I'm done folks. See you tomorrow."

I went home and sprawled out on the new couch in the new screenroom.

Boy, was I glad to get out of that conference. I'm beat! I'm glad to get home, sit down and kick off my shoes, and make some coffee or tea. The tea sounds better because its cool. I'll just sit for a few minutes.

I haven't talked to Norm or Earl yet, they always make me smile and feel good. Where's that phone?

I decided to call Earl first. I wanted to see how he liked that old run-down pickup we gave him. No Answer. I'll just drive over there to his house.

Earl was in his shop working on another stained glass superlative. I don't know how he does it, but the finished product speaks for itself.

When I started helping him with this glass business he has, the panels were weighing about thirty or forty pounds and I could easily handle them. Now I'm sure they must be weighing seventy or eighty pounds. He must be adding lead or something to them. I'm having trouble carrying them now. The glass must be getting heavy for him too, but he never complains about it.

Earl was working on a project, but when I walked in, he stopped and acted like I did him a favor by stopping him.

It takes hours and hours to make one of these things. I could not be still that long. He told me that the last one he did when I was in his shop had eighteen hundred and some pieces.

I have found that he would rather do the big, even huge, projects than something in a person's house. We have done a few houses, but they never have protective covering over the windows. Sometimes there are storm windows over them, a hail storm that would break the stained glass window, would totally destroy a storm window.

"Well, DJ! What can I do for you?" he said.

"Let's go for a ride."

Earl wanted to drive, so I left my car at his house. Earl drove over to Norm's shop in that brand-new old 1949 pickup we gave him and he smiled every inch of the way.

It was so clean, I wondered if I should take off my shoes when I rode in it.

Norm was in his shop and busy with two of his guys working on another old car. They didn't notice us, so we just walked around like we were in a shopping center. There was an old '55 Olds Rocket, and a '56 Desoto Fireflite. I haven't seen a Desoto in years.

Norm finally found us and we stood and talked about his work and the cars. Norm has a funny streak, but no one ever sees it unless he really goes over the edge. But he surprised me with this next one.

"You know, Earl, since you're the stained glass man, you could put a stained glass window in that old Dodge Caravan that you drive." He said.

I about choked trying not to laugh at that last comment. I made a point to look at Norm to see if he was smiling, but he wasn't. He couldn't have been serious, could he?

"Sure! You could make it the rear window on the driver's side. The driver can't look through that window anyway." Norm said.

"I think I like that! You might have a great idea there, Norm." Earl said.

That took me by surprise. I can tell its time to go. You don't suppose that Earl would do that?

Earl only stayed a few more minutes and we were off again to somewhere new. After about four or five more stops, I finally got home and collapsed on the couch. This is beginning to be a habit.

When I left DC, I told Martin that he could call me when he had something solid that we could chew on.

I just hate it when I say something like that and it boomerangs back at me. The next day I was having breakfast with my beautiful wife when the phone rang and she handed it to me. It was Lopez.

I hadn't been comfortable for ten minutes when the phone rang. I just know this is not good news.

"Could you come down to my office? We're going to have a conference call at ten o'clock." Lopez said.

I dressed and grudgingly drove slowly to the office. My car doesn't like 'slow'.

When the call came in, Lopez put it on speaker and we listened as Martin and Olson and my Director told us how to do what they wanted us to do.

"Who are we looking for? This guy Clayton? He must be important"

"He is! And we want you guys to bring him in." He said. "Alive! If possible."

"Why me?"

"Because you're fearless." He said.

"You mean that if I'm afraid I wouldn't have to go on these stupid outings all over the country for you?"

"Well, that's pretty crass, but, yes, I don't have anyone who can do what you do, the way that you do it. But they don't have as many bodies left behind like you do." He said.

"Would it do any good to say 'I'm afraid'?"

"Not a bit. We know your history."

"Damn! If I shoot him, can we go home?"

We all laughed about that one, but none of them did.

"They all have a protection detail and you don't" The Director said.

"Oh, man! I suppose that we are expected to show up in DC after all this is done, too?"

"Correct. I see that you're beginning to think like a politician now." He said.

"Not a compliment!"

"Did you find out any more about this mysterious Congressman, Martin?"

"DJ, you won't believe what this guy's name is." Martin said.

"OK, I give up."

"Hilliard Clayton." He said.

"Come on, that's not even a real name."

"Yes it is. It's German."

"German? German people aren't terrorists."

"Why not? We have records on almost all the terrorists and they are a mix of every nationality, language, background and religion there is." He said.

"Well then, we better find this Hilliard Clayton and his gang right away.

"We have information that he is in Missouri, someplace called Trenton, and we know that you and all your friends know Missouri. We've been looking in New Jersey. I didn't know about a town in Missouri called Trenton. You can bring in Mike and Ted and any others if you want." He said.

Well it looks like we have six people to perform for the audience. Jim was already in the room when the call came in. I called Mike and Ted, and asked them to call their very close friends, Jake and Ron. Martin brought an FBI friend named Angelo Pessetto and Olson brought an unnamed friend, no doubt CIA.

I think that the only reason they wanted us to help them was that none of them knew anything about Missouri. We were assigned one leader to each of four teams.

I got Angelo. He's from New Jersey. And he talks funny. He couldn't understand me and I couldn't understand him. We laughed all day every day. And we found a few troublemakers, but Clayton was our target. We all started in Trenton, a town of about seven thousand. Nothing there.

The northern part of the state went pretty quickly, but there's a lot of farm land and farmers and I'm sure the terrorists don't want to be bothered with them. I know the farmers don't have any interest in them either.

Farmers don't have the time or the patience to put up with some crazy guy talking politics and hate. So the crazies stay mostly to the bigger towns.

We have made squares all over the state, and we meet once a week in the nearest big town to compare notes We found a lot of drug dealers and their customers, but alas, no Hilliard Clayton.

We got Columbia and Jefferson City. I was sure that we would be overloaded with bad guys from there. It was surprisingly mostly clean. There's all those politicians in Jeff City, and I expected we'd find a lot of blood suckers hanging around.

One of our stops was in Rolla. Angelo and I sat at the counter and when the waitress brought our coffee, I laid my folder with the photos down.

The waitress picked up one of the photos and said. "This guy was in here yesterday. Are you looking for him?"

"Yes! Do you know him?"

"No, he was just a customer, but he was acting funny. Like he had some kind of an itch." She said.

"Where was the itch?"

"Most of the time, he was scratching his chest and belly. But I saw a little red sore on his neck too." She said.

"OK. I've got it all. Would you give me your contact info so I can get back to you if I need to?"

"Sure." She took her pen and wrote her name, address and phone number on her order pad and tore off the sheet and gave it to me.

I knew that I needed to talk to Martin about this. I don't know what he was scratching, but now he has an identifier and we had better spread the word quickly.

Angelo and I spent two weeks lounging around Missouri and by the time we hit the Arkansas border we were whipped. We contacted Martin and explained where we would be for the next few days and beat a path to our homes. It's always nice to know that the FBI knows where I am.

I like Angelo, we could work together again.

Chapter 13

The Congressman

After all the grueling travel around the state of Missouri and all the walking, talking, running and coffee was finished, I was glad to have a little time to talk to Ted about money.

"Ted, I think we've been going at this the wrong way. I bet that if we find the money, we'll find Clayton right in with it."

"I think you're right. But where do we start?" He said.

"We've done counterfeiting before. This guy can't be any smarter than the others we've dealt with."

"I have a few ideas. Let me see what I can find." He said.

"I wonder if he would have started a Foundation."

"Hey! You might just have hit it on the head. If he did, I can get a lot of good news." He said.

"What can I do?"

"Well! Where does the money come from? Where does it go? What has he bought in the last few years? I'll bet he drives a big fancy car." He said.

"Anything else?"

"You know those guys at the Federal Reserve. See what they can tell us. Find out that if we can prove he's a crook, can we get his money back to the Treasury." He said.

"I'll call you when I have something. I'm going home. It's time to unwind."

It doesn't take me long to find something I like when I get back home and have a chance to enjoy it. Denise designed and had this screenroom built and I like it. Not as much as I like her and the kids, but it's right up there.

Jason really went overboard with the room. He did the best work I had ever seen. I especially like the fold-up hammock that he put in.

We spent the rest of that week and the weekend together before any of us wanted to do something else. The girls had a big time cooking all the meals and showing off some new recipes. They really love that outdoor kitchen.

On Monday morning I asked Ann Webster to help me find Emerson's money and anything else he might own. She was glad to help.

Ted called and told me all about a foundation that he found with Clayton's name all over it.

"So Clayton and Emerson were in business together? It looks like all we have to do is find them. Sounds easy doesn't it? But it never is!"

After Ted called, I contacted my friend at the Federal Reserve Bank in Salt Lake.

"Good morning Alex. I have a couple questions for you. We are currently chasing a guy who is involved in counterfeiting and might have a foundation where he stores the profits of his business. If we prove he is a crook, can we confiscate and return all of his money to the Treasury?"

"Well, the first answer is yes. You may confiscate the money in the foundation, if you can prove that the money was obtained from a criminal enterprise. Second, the money in the foundation would go back to those who were harmed in the criminal enterprise. Anyone who put money into it and were not participating in crime would be those who were harmed." He said.

"We found that he did not have a foundation before he was involved with others who we are hunting for the same crimes. And by the way the foundation was started after Clayton was elected."

"It sounds like the money could go to the Treasury then. But you have a lot of work to do to prove that." He said.

I wasn't off the phone to Salt Lake for a minute, when there was another call from the Director and Martin.

"I have something about the foundation and the counterfeit money."

"The only counterfeit was in twenty dollar bills." He said.

"By the way, we found out what he was scratching. Our doctor thinks it could be Shingles. It would be very hard to hide it. This disease makes red welts on the face and neck, chest and stomach. It also produces severe pain and itching."

I was smiling the whole time Martin was telling me about Emerson's problem.

"And it's serious. He could die from this disease." Martin said.

"If he does, then I wouldn't have to shoot him." I said and laughed a little.

They never seem to get my humor.

"We want him back alive so we can question him. He might know something important." He said.

"Isn't it time that you came in to the office and let us see your smiling face?' The Director said.

I got the message loud and clear. Ted was very happy to get the plane ready ad fly to DC again. For the hundredth time I think.

So here we are landing at our favorite Maryland airport. Now here we are riding in a fancy car toward Washington DC with Jerry, our favorite driver, but not my favorite town.

After we were finished with our coffee break, Jerry, Ted and I walked back to his office. I noticed that there was a man following us. But there are so many people in the Big House, that that's pretty normal. Jerry has a folder in his hand with 'TS' on it. Again pretty normal because of the location.

Suddenly the man comes running toward us and grabbed the folder from Jerry's hand and pushed Ted and him to the floor. That made me mad. He went running down the hall toward the exit doors.

One of the WH guards tackled him and the TS folder went sliding on the newly waxed floor toward us.

"Quick! Pick up the folder. I don't want my prints on it." I yelled at Jerry.

Andy had the cuffs on the guy before he knew it.

Jerry grabbed the folder before anyone showed up. It only took a few seconds before we were overcome with people. White House Security were there first and they helped Jerry, Ted and I to our feet.

Now comes the questions.

It seemed like everyone in the hallway was talking at once and asking the same questions. I did not know any of the answers and fortunately all of them were directed at Jerry. He is, after all, the only one that any of them knew. And I have one of my disguises on, so I'm nobody.

There was a hall full of people, almost before we could get our bearings. One of the guards helped us up and pulled me out of traffic and we talked quietly.

"What was that all about, DJ?" He asked.

"I saw this guy in the cafeteria when we were having coffee, but never before. He followed us out into the hall, but I didn't give it any notice, because there are so many people milling around."

"Who is he?. I wonder why he would want that folder? Andy said.

"Let's get his wallet and find his name."

Andy bent over him and searched all his pockets.

"No wallet. Nothing in any of his pockets but lint. Nice shoes. Clean clothes. Clean T shirt and his shirt and tie are cleaned and pressed. Not much to go on here." Andy said.

"Well, the folder does say "TS", maybe he was going to sell it. Or maybe he might be a terrorist. I like that answer better."

"I wonder if he was working alone?" He said.

"Ask him. Don't talk to us. We don't know anything, but I could question him. I might even enjoy that."

"No! No! I've heard about your brand of questioning." He said.

"Maybe you should start taking photos of all of these people. We could have a lucky break."

His phone flew into his hand and we had half of them on film almost before I finished the sentence.

Ted had been taking photos of everyone from the moment he fell on the floor. He is, after all, the smartest guy around and would think of that before any of us.

"His shoes don't show any wear. I wonder if he hasn't worn them before. I'm going to check to see what store sells them. Maybe someone will remember something. Can you get them for me?"

Andy had his gloves on and the shoes came off in his hands. I had a bag with me and they disappeared.

Two guys with a gurney took the guy away while Andy was waving his phone/camera around. I assume there is a place to keep him till the medics get here. I hope we got a photo of someone good for us.

I got a phone book and Ted and I copied the pages with all the shoe stores listed. Sometimes you have to assume things. I assumed that this guy didn't buy these shoes downtown. He probably made a special trip out to a hard to find store at the edge of town.

I visited several stores until I was dealt a huge surprise. At each store I introduced myself, showed my badge and told the clerk what I was looking for and why.

Finally I struck gold. Bart, the clerk, told me about the sale.

"Why, yes. I remember those shoes. I sold them just a few days ago. Let me get the receipt. - - - Here it is." He said.

"What makes you remember them so quickly?"

"They were bought by a woman." He said.

"They were bought by a woman?"

"Yes. That's why I remember it so well. No woman I have ever met wears a size twelve man's brogan." He said.

"Can you describe her for me?"

"Sure. About late thirties or early forties, medium height about five five or so, brown hair, jeans and sweatshirt, no purse or hat, nothing special. She looked normal or average. Sorry, best I can do." He said.

"Do you have her name, I hope?"

"No. She paid in cash. But she left the box. She took them out in a plastic bag." He said.

"Maybe I could take the box and get a fingerprint from it. Would you mind if I took it?"

"Not at all." He said.

"Be careful. Don't touch it if you can help it. I have gloves."

We put the box in a plastic bag and was very careful with it. I took the box and what little info I had back to Martin and he took the shoe box in the bag.

Later, I finally had a few minutes to talk to Martin while we were having a cup of coffee and trying to shake off the effects of the last little bit of fun.

We talked about the guy, his shoes, an unknown woman, all the pictures that were taken, why the folder. And more importantly, how did he get into the White House?

Andy had his and the other guard's phone photos made into prints for us. We scoured them with magnifying glasses for people that were out of place or moving around. We found four. Andy took all the pix to the shop and had the four people enlarged to eight by tens so we could see them better.

None of us interviewed any of them. Jerry recognized one woman.

"Hey, I know this one. She works at State. I'll check on her." He said.

Jerry was back in only a few minutes with some bad news. The woman in the photo was in good standing at State and was not the one we want.

Jerry and I rounded up all the pictures and we ran back to the shoe store.

"Excuse me Bart, I have some pictures I would like you to look at for us."

He took the handful of pictures and began dealing them out on the table like playing cards as he went through them.

"That's her! Not one of these big ones. There standing in the back of this one." Bart said and handed me the photo and pointed out the woman.

He was right. She is as normal looking as anyone. You wouldn't even recognize her if you didn't know her for a while.

Martin called me back a few days later. They couldn't identify the lone fingerprint they found on the shoe box. It was not in the files.

Chapter 14

We Catch The Crooks

We didn't find out who called with the tip, but we know that Clayton and Emerson are the terrorists and the counterfeiters.

We need to find his secretary and the two aides.

Ted and I drove over to the House Office Building and found the secretary working away in Clayton's office. We had better interview her before we leave to go to Little Rock.

"Can you tell me what you do for the Congressman here?"

"Yes. I answer the phone and the mail. I am always helping any visitors with meetings and comments, and making sure the Congressman is present for any votes or meetings. Basically I am arranging his schedule." She said.

"I've heard a lot of talk about the sexual assaults. Does that happen with him?"

"No assaults. He tells me what he wants to do and we do it."

"Are you married or have a boyfriend?"

"Yes, I have a boyfriend. We do the same thing. He tells me what he wants to do and we do it."

"Where were you born?"

"Right here in DC." She said.

"Why did you go to work for Clayton?"

"He asked around for a secretary who didn't like country music, and I was hired. He hates the music and the people in that part of the country too." She said.

"Why doesn't he like them?"

"He said that they want everything." She said.

"Like what?"

"Like clean water." She said.

"You would think that everyone would want clean water. That's silly. Besides, we already have it. Here at the sink."

"But he said that it's processed there. He said that nobody wants processed water. He says that nobody believes that the people should work for what they want. He feels that the Government should raise taxes and give stuff to the people for free." She said.

"Like what stuff?"

"Everything. Food, schooling, housing, transportation, cars, everything that people need and want." She said.

"I wonder where he would have heard that kind of baloney?"

I looked at Ted and he just shrugged his shoulders.

"What about his two aides?"

"They feel the same way as he does." She said. "But they are a lot more vocal about it."

"Do you know where they are from?"

"I can look it up for you." She said.

She looked on her computer for the personnel records.

"It says here that both of his aides came from Lebanon." She said.

"Do you know where Clayton and the rest are now?"

"I heard something about a music show or concert." She said.

"So that's why Emerson is going to Arkansas."

We all met at city hall in Little Rock. They told us where the concert and the political rally were going to be.

Martin passed out blue jackets with big yellow letters that say FBI on the back for us.

"Wow, look at me, I'm in the FBI."

We all laughed at my joke and went to work. It wasn't far to the location where the concert would be presented. We decided to walk so we could get the feel of the location and surrounding area.

The concert started right on time and the crowds were filling up the building as well as the parking lot and streets close by. People had flags and hats and every kind of patriotic thing you could imagine.

A few minutes after the music began, I noticed one of Clayton's aides standing in the middle of the crowd. I don't know why, but I took the time to completely examine him. Then I noticed that he was carrying a pistol.

"BAMG" "BANG"

"Martin! The shooters are in the crowd. Clayton's aides. I see one of them with a pistol, looks like a 1911-A1. I'm going after him!"

"BANG" "BANG" "BANG" "BANG"

I caught up to him just as he began to unload his clip. I ran up behind him and put two in his back and he fell like a bag of rocks.

"Physstt" Physstt"

People began to scream and run away. Then as if by magic the crowd cleared away from the other aide.

"BANG" "BANG" "BANG"

I ran to get the 45 the first one was carrying. He saw me and raised his pistol to fire at me, but was just a half second too slow.

"BANG"

I put two in his chest.

"Physstt" Physstt"

I wanted to make a matching set. I picked up his 45 too and put them both in the pockets of the blue jacket.

"BANG" "BANG" "BANG"

There was lots of yelling and screaming, and people running in all directions.

"BANG" "BANG"

"Martin! I got both of the aides, but Emerson and maybe Clayton are still here. We've got to find them, and fast. This is getting out of control."

"BANG" "BANG"

I jumped up onto the stage and grabbed the microphone on the support at the front of the stage and yelled into it.

"BANG" "BANG"

"Whoever is running the lights, I need a spotlight on the crowd to find the shooter! Fast!"

"BANG" "BANG"

The huge spot came on and began sweeping the crowd. Suddenly it stopped and I saw Emerson. I could tell he was in pain, but he had his pistol and was waving it around. He was firing it but his arms weren't working the way he wanted and the bullets were mostly going up into the air. I'll bet he never fired a 45 before.

The light lit up Emerson holding his pistol and he saw me.

"I hate you!

"Yeah! Yeah! Get in line!"

"You Americans think you are better than us!" He yelled.

"That's because we are!" I yelled back.
Emerson took careful aim and fired.

"BANG"

But his pistol was pointing straight up. Too bad.
I kneeled down on one knee and took my hundred
yard shot and he dropped like a stone.

"Physstt"

Most of the crowd saw my shot and Emerson fall.
I walked down and picked up his pistol and stuck
it in one of the pockets with the others. The crowd
sounded like it heaved a sigh of relief.

I went back to the stage and picked up the microphone again.

"Thanks light man, You helped us out a lot. If
you'll come see me, I'd like to shake your hand."

A few seconds later, the Little Rock Police were
swarming in all the doors and the people began to
calm down a little.

One cop saw my blue jacket and he came over to
talk to me.

"What happened here?" He asked.

"We've been tracking a ring of terrorists who hate
everyone. We found out that they were planning to
kill everyone here at the concert. Our group inter-
ceded before they could complete their task. There
must be a few bodies around, a lot of shots were
fired. We got at least four of them. I picked up a few
pistols."

"Martin Butcher is the boss here. You'll see him with one of our jackets on. There are a few more of us. We'll be clearing out very soon. It's all yours now." I saw Martin walking toward us. "There's Martin now."

As we were standing there, a woman with a cell phone came to us and said. "I saw this man all dressed up in an expensive black suit and tie and was walking through the crowd and shooting people for no reason. I took a couple pictures of him if you want them."

"You bet I do!"

"Here! I can transfer them to your phone." She said, and she did.

"Will you need to know my name and address?" She asked.

"I sure would appreciate that."

She was very cooperative and would make a good witness if we need her.

I pointed out Martin and we walked to where he was. I handed Martin the pistols that I had found and walked away.

The officer introduced himself as a Lieutenant of the local PD.

I saw Mike and Brown coming our way and went to meet them.

"Martin's talking to the Little Rock cops, so I vote we exit the area."

"I agree." Brown said. "I've had enough fun for one day."

We moved as secretly as possible toward a door and successfully got out without being noticed. I had my blue jacket off and on the back of a chair long before we found the door. None of us are going back to DC now. It's time to go home.

One of the photos from the woman at the concert shows Clayton holding the pistol and fire coming out of the barrel. How convenient!

"This should be the last nail in his coffin!"

Chapter 15

What Bomb?

Just as we were finishing up, one of the FBI guys saw a man running, carrying a gun and a remote. The FBI guy yelled. "Get him!"

Ted, Mike, and I all ran after him. He made one mistake. He turned to shoot at us and all three of us shot at him.

"BANG."

"BANG." "BANG." "Physstt."

Ted and Mike grabbed him, and Ted got the remote and Mike took the gun.

"The remote might be a bomb, I'll take care of it." Ted said.

"It looks like he might live. Only one of you hit him." Martin said.

"Too bad!"

Mike put the leg irons on him and I did the hand cuffs and the FBI carried him away. They presented him to the Little Rock Police, and Ted took the remote apart and stuck it in his pocket. All of this took less that a couple of minutes. The news people came in with the police but they missed this one.

It was a regular madhouse there. The news people had to call all of the state officials. There had been no time between the time of the concert and the time that the news people showed up. It's like they were waiting outside for something to happen. I wonder if they had been tipped off.

None of the state officials had been notified that there was an attack. They were doing other things when it happened and the news people wanted to shock them with the news first.

During the interviews at the concert hall, TV stations and networks were fighting over who gets to talk to who first. It's almost a joke, they interrupt each other and try to talk over each other.

'I'm more important than you!' seems to be the theme of the day.

News people don't bother with ordinary people, they sent their people to hunt down the Arkansas Governor, Senator and Representatives for TV interviews. When they get the video tapes of these interviews back to their studios, they will slant every word to suit themselves, truth or not.

By the time the Governor and the others got there, he had been briefed on the situation. The Governor handled the media's questions with am amazing amount of finesse and subtlety. Another unsung genius.

One bigmouth reporter said that he wants to let Clayton go free. He went on with a comment that because Clayton was a Congressman how could he ever take part of a thing like this. I grabbed him and we had a little talk out of earshot of the cameras. He decided to change his mind and not talk about it. And I told him he could not attend another of these press conferences. He really wanted to argue, but there I was. I made sure to get a picture of him and his press card.

The next day, the Director called me and wanted a report on what happened in Little Rock. I've never been good at giving a report over the phone, but he insisted.

"We found out that the Congressman was the leader of the terrorist cell in Danbury, Connecticut. His right hand man was Emerson. There were two Congressional Aides. They are related and came here from Lebanon. Others in the family also came. We think there are seventeen. His secretary is a distant cousin whose parents came to America years ago. She was born in DC."

"We found another of their relatives working in DC. He was an aide to another Congressman and only saw Clayton's people in passing. But that was only for show. They were together very often. We got him too."

"During the shoot-out at the concert, we got ten of the terrorists, including Emerson. The secretary is working somewhere in DC. The two aides were eliminated at the concert. That leaves three of them to find."

"What about Clayton?" He asked.

"We don't know where he is. But I have a photo taken by a girl at the concert that shows him firing a gun with the fire coming out of the barrel. There is another that shows who he shot. I think he is a prime candidate for Gitmo, I'll even volunteer to take him there."

"No. Because I know what would happen if you were the one transporting him there. In addition, I had a report that a newsman says he saw Clayton somewhere else and not at the concert." He said.

"That's a lie! I have the photos. I could send them to you. The reporter could be working with him. We've found a couple more people who were, one of them is a banker. He probably has a picture that was taken last week. I'm going to need to know who that newsman is. We can't leave any stone unturned."

"OK! Send me the photo. I'll get it in the paper and they can scream all they want." He said.

"Before you go sir, I'd like to give an award to the guy who did the lights at the concert. He did us a great favor and may have kept me from being shot. I made it a point to meet him. We shook hands and talked about body count, he said he saw bodies all over the floor from where he was. I gave him my card with the phone number, and promised to help if he needed anything."

"Send me some facts. I'll need his name and what he did for us. Don't worry, I'll make it happen." He said.

Chapter 16

Who Wants To Be On Television?

A long time ago, I went to see my friend James Tru-
jillo when he was running for Mayor. 'WhaddaYa
Know Joe' was on TV and the radio almost every
day and he was going to interview Jim the next day.
It was set up to be in the parking lot of the Citadel
Shopping Center.

Jim asked me to come just for the security. He was
a little worried about something. I said sure and told
him I would wear a disguise in case there was any
trouble.

The disguise I wore was gray hair, a mustache,
bushy eyebrows, high cheeks, and brown skin. It
worked fine and I got the guy who was threatening
Jim. He went to jail for a few years. He's probably
out by now.

I haven't seen Joe on TV in years, but after all this
craziness for the last several months, I decided to
drop in on him unannounced and scare him a little. I
needed a little fun.

"And now the 'WhaddaYa Know, Joe' Show, star-
ring Joe!" The announcer said in a loud boisterous
voice.

Joe came out on stage through the curtains and
did his monologue and walked to the host's chair
and table.

"And now Ladies and Gentlemen our first guest. A famous Hollywood actor, Clark Gable!" The announcer said.

The curtains opened and out walked a middle aged man with black hair and dressed in a fine looking tuxedo. He walked to the seat next to the host of the show and said. "Hello, Joe, Whadda ya know?" Then I laughed and sat down.

"You're not Clark Gable! Who are you?" Joe asked.

"No, I'm not Clark Gable. He's been gone for years. I just wanted to get your attention."

"My name is DJ. You probably don't remember our first meeting. It was a long time ago. You were interviewing a candidate for Mayor, James Trujillo. He is a long time friend of mine, and he called me then to provide some protection for that interview."

"You're DJ? The man who was identified as DJ to me was old and wrinkled with gray hair and dirty clothes." Joe said.

"That was just a disguise as this one is now. I wanted to be close to the Mayor in case anything did actually happen. And it did, as you may remember."

"You're wearing a disguise right now?" He asked.

"You don't think I look like this all the time do you?"

The audience laughed a little.

"Sorry, I couldn't tell." He said.

His face got a little red, but he went on.

"What did you do?" He asked.

"When the Mayor called me he told me that he had been getting threatening phone calls and cut-out letters from someone. We checked with all our sources and found this guy who hated him and you."

"Why did he hate me?" Joe said.

"We never found out, and I didn't know he was to be taken alive."

"They have to tell you ahead of time?" He said.

"Well, yes, of course. If someone is threatening people with death I figure it's only fair to do the same for them."

His mouth dropped open and his face really got red then.

"I hear that you are dangerous." He said.

The audience went "ooo and aaah'.

"I've been told that a time or two. But don't believe everything you hear. It's not always true. I'm a really sweet guy."

I had to laugh along with the audience with that one. He smiled but didn't seem to get the joke.

"Why are you here now?" He said.

"We've been out hunting terrorists and we caught a cell of them recently. It was time for us to take a break from this kind of work.   But I'm still searching for one man in particular."

"Oh! You're talking about a criminal called One Shot McCoy. I understand everyone has hunted him for a long time." He said. "And you can't find him?"

"No. He has the ability to change his appearance any time he wants."

"What do you do?" He asked.

"I'm in in a strange business called Law Enforcement. You may have heard of it."

I laughed and he chuckled a little.

"So you carry a gun? He asked.

"Yes sir."

"All the time?" He asked.

"Every day, all day long."

"Can I see it?" He asked.

"No sir."

"Why not? Just a simple answer."

"Because if I brought it out for you to see, all the cameras in the world would have photos of it with me waving it around like a crazy man and I would be on the front page of every paper with video on every TV station saying that I was attacking you or someone on your show and I should be arrested for terrorism or treason and put in jail for life or executed."

"Is that a simple enough answer?"

He seemed shocked that I would say such a thing to him about his people. And on TV too.

"What kind is it?"

"Sorry, same answer. If I said it is a revolver, the reporters would change it to a semi, and if I said I was a semi, then. Well you know."

"You don't like the Media?"

"NO! I love the Media! They help us in a lot of ways. But I hate liars. And I have run across more than one reporter who will build a huge lie about someone they don't even know out of nothing while sitting at their desk in their plush little chair, in hopes that it will make them seem more important or more famous."

"And they call us liars and all the other names they can think of."

"I even talked to a famous TV anchor who didn't know about the biggest and most famous jail in this country in a little town near Kansas City.

"Oh, you mean Leavenworth." He said.

"How hard was that?"

"I see that you have quite a sense of humor."

"Not when it comes to defending this country. I told one guy the he wouldn't like me when I'm angry. He tried to be a smart-ass and said that I was trying to be the Big Hulk. I showed him what the Big Hulk might do and he shut his mouth. - - - - For a long time."

"Have you shot any terrorists?" He asked.

"One or two."

"I just stopped by to say 'Hi'. And now a word from our sponsor."

The lights went down and I scurried out the back and onto the street where we had a car and my favorite driver, Mike, waiting. I changed my jacket and removed parts of the disguise and we drove away.

"One or two?" Mike said. "Does that mean every day?"

We both laughed for the rest of the drive to my house. Mike and Sally came for a visit after the Little Rock escapade. We all needed some down time.

When the commercial was completed and they were back to Joe, someone asked "Who was that?"

"A man who saved my life many years ago and who he is or what he looks like, I don't know. I have never seen his face." Joe said.

"Can you tell us about it?" His announcer said.

"I was doing an exterior interview with a candidate for the Mayor. Some guy came through the crowd and tried to shoot me and the Mayor. DJ came behind him and when the guy raised his gun to shoot us, DJ hit him with his cane. The guy spun around and pointed his gun at DJ. That's when DJ shot him." Joe said.

"DJ looked like an old guy with a gray beard, scraggly hair and old clothes with a cane."

"When the cops came, they grabbed DJ and took him to a squad car. A few minutes later I saw him walking around without the cops holding him."

"He was dressed nothing like he was tonight. I don't know his name or who he works for. I haven't seen him again until now." Joe said.

The TV show was a hoot, but I can do without that kind of stuff in my life. Joe will probably talk about that for a long time now.

I like to sit down with Norm and just talk about nothing at all. We both like cars and the law and God. So our discussions are sometimes very long and very different from most people.

"You know, we have talked about almost everything, but you have never said anything about your close encounters with death. You said there were some, but that's as far as you went with it. I sure would like to hear the rest." Norm said.

"OK! You asked for it. Get ready!"

Chapter 17

A Real Miracle

The dictionary definition of a Miracle is this. 'A wonderful happening that is contrary to or independent of the known laws of nature.'

We had been in Wichita for quite a few years when we both decided it was time to go back home to Colorado Springs. We both set about to do all the work to be ready to go. It was a long arduous process.

I was the Logistics Management Officer and I worked for a full Colonel. I begged him to find a place for me to go in the Springs area, I told him that I would take anything, but I couldn't take cancer again. I was told by the oncologist that Kansas is the number one state in the country for Lymphoma. In a few months, he found a place for me at the Air Force Academy.

I was driving a 1974 Porsche 914 and my wife had a big Chrysler New Yorker. We also had a full size Dodge van that we used for trips to see her family in Missouri. But now we needed something to haul all the extras that people accumulate and want to keep forever.

I found a big straight truck with a van body at a bread company and bought it for the move. I built shelves in it and loaded boxes till I thought I couldn't carry them anymore. We sold or gave away all our furniture but a few very special pieces.

Now we have four vehicles and only two drivers. Something had to be done to relieve the stress.

During the time we waited for the transfer, my friend Mike and I built a special little trailer for the race car to be transported on. I had too many vehicles and too few drivers.

Since the Porsche 914 is a very small and light car, it didn't need to be a big brawny trailer. We loaded the car with gas and oil and all the necessary fluids and strapped it securely to the trailer with trucker straps. Then we parked it in a secure place until I could come back and transport it home. I would use the big van to do the job.

We moved back to the Springs in November. We bought a house and got my wife, her car, the bread truck full of her valuables and the special pieces and parts, that could be hauled in the van, moved soon after that.

Then in March of the next year I took the big Dodge van back to Wichita and hooked up the trailer with the car loaded on it and began the five hundred mile trip back to the Springs. Once I had the trailer attached, wired and chained to the van, I was on my way.

From Wichita, the trip goes out US 54 through Kingman, Pratt, Greensburg, and Dodge City to US 50. Then on to Garden City, the Kansas Border, and Lamar Colorado.

I normally listen to 106.3 on the FM dial when I'm home, but I was too far away for that. I picked up a station in southern Colorado and the weatherman was describing a storm coming in from the south west. He didn't make it sound too bad. And it wasn't up to the front range as yet.

We call these storms an 'Albuquerque Low'. There are two tracks that these storms normally follow. One is that they stay south of Interstate Forty and sweep across Texas and Oklahoma. The other is when the storm grabs the Rockies and takes a hard left and travels north along the front range.

These are the dangerous ones. Since the mountains are a wall and the storm is twisting into the wall it will travel north through the three major cities in the state and end up in Wyoming. They also carry a lot of snow with them, since these are winter storms.

I decided on making the turn north on US 287 toward Kit Carson. This would put me another fifty miles or more away from any weather, I thought. At Kit Carson, I made the turn west on Highway 94. Highway 94 is as straight as a string to the Springs from Kit Carson and you can see Pikes Peak grow up out of the horizon as you go. There are a few little towns there but mostly prairie.

Kit Carson is about a hundred miles east of the Springs, and the radio said the storm was down around Walsenburg south west of Pueblo and not into the mountains yet. I thought it would miss the area where I would be driving.

By the time I arrived at Punkin Center, it was beginning to rain. It was a light rain, but it was raining harder as I went west. I didn't see this as threatening and I continued on to Rush but I slowed down to about fifty MPH. It was beginning to snow in Yoder, not much, but the wind had come up pretty hard. I was slowing down my speed all the way along.

But in Ellicott the snow was coming down sideways in sheets and heavy winds were driving it. By this time I was only making about twenty MPH. I had driven into a full blown blizzard. A blizzard is just a hurricane with snow.

I thought if I could get down 'trash hill' to the bottom of the valley, the wind and bad stuff would be blowing above me and when I would come up on the other side I would be in town at the entrance to Peterson Field.

But by the time I approached the top of "trash hill" the wind was so severe that a huge gust put me in the ditch head first. Once the van stopped and the motor shut itself off, I took the keys and put them in my pocket. The dog house was packed full of snow and I wasn't going anywhere in that van.

Two thoughts came to mind. One, I can't stay here, it's too cold, I would freeze. Two, I had better get walking, it's about ten miles to my house, and it's very dark and cold out there. I had been driving since yesterday and exhaustion was coming on strong.

Walking ten miles in a blizzard isn't smart, but it looked like the only option.

So, what to do? Get out of the van and assess the situation. Fortunately, I had a warm coat and sweater on with heavy socks and boots.

As I walked to the back of the van, I found the little red Porsche sitting in the middle of the road on all four tires with no damage to any part of it. Not even a scratch!

It said to me, "Hi, would you like a ride?"

With the wind howling and the snow pelting me like BB's being shot at me, I decided to get into the car and take my chances.

It started easily and when I put it in first gear and let the clutch out I began to move down the hill very slowly. Since the car had a very low profile, the wind didn't move it as much as the van.

I found that twenty miles per hour in second gear was a good speed to plow through the snow which was piling up quickly and resist the wind. I was careful to stay in the middle of the road. I can't afford to go in the ditch here.

It was a slow ride through the 'white out' but soon I was on Platte Avenue and a city was growing up around me. I did not see another car on any of the streets of the city as I trudged toward my house. People are really smart after all.

I was careful to park the car in a little niche with the garage in front of me and a big wooden fence on the north of me. When I entered the house, my wife was shocked, worried, excited and happy all at the same time.

Now I have a question for you. How do you think that the car, which was strapped securely to the trailer, came off of the trailer in that blizzard wind and snow and landed on all four of its tires without sustaining any damage at all? Not even a scratch.

There could only be three ways to get that car from the trailer onto the paved road.

One, you could use the ramps you used to drive it on with and drive it off after all the straps were removed. But the ramps were undisturbed.

Two, you could wreck the trailer and turn it over. The heavy load then would be crashed on it's top or side and be unusable. But the car was undamaged.

Three, someone with a crane could lift it off from above. But there was no one or any kind of equipment to be seen.

I couldn't have driven it off the trailer, I was in the van. I am sure there was no one near there as far as I could see.

So, what do you think was the reason for all of this? Coincidence? Luck? Fate? In the right place at the right time? Maybe an Angel lifted it off of the trailer for me.

I like that last answer but I've always heard that angels were about the size of a butterfly. If it was an angel, he would be the size of a tractor trailer to lift that car.

How many ways can we describe God's Hand by not saying it?

There can be only one answer.

I don't know why He saved me, but He did. I have always heard that these kinds of things happen because He has something more for us to do in our life. I hope I'm doing it.

One thing about miracles, you can't pray for them if you don't know you need them. And, by the time that you do need it, it is too late to pray for it.

For God did not give us a spirit of fear, but a spirit of power, of love and of self-discipline.

Chapter 18

A Visit To The House

"I called the Speaker and briefed him on what we were doing. We need to get to the House Chamber and arrest this clown before he gets away. Let's Go!" Martin said.

"What's with these people? Why do they want to kill everyone?" Mike asked.

"I've studied this terrorism idea that they have. They believe that every form of regulation or government is immoral! That restraint of any one person is an evil which must be destroyed! But they themselves do this everyday and in their minds it is the will of God to kill all other people that do not believe what they believe. Much like a lot of our own people in this country."

"What we are going to do today in Congress is what the people who wrote the Constitution had in mind for this kind of problem." Martin said. "You can find it all in Article three, Section three."

The Speaker called me a few minutes later on my phone and said that I should listen carefully and not tell anyone what you are doing.

"I would like for you to show up with Agent Butcher and his friends. I want you to be dressed in a very special uniform. Jeans, dirty if possible, tee shirt and long-sleeve flannel shirt, any kind of dirty hat or cap, and an old jacket. You can pick all this stuff up at the thrift shop just a few blocks away. I'll have Jerry take you and bring you back or take you to the hotel."

"Now here's what I want you to do."

He explained in great detail what he wanted.

"When the time is right, I'll call on you and use the name 'One Shot' so you will know that it's time for your performance. What do you think of that?" He said.

"I love it. I'll scare the wits out of that guy so bad he won't be able to go outside without being afraid that someone will shoot him. We still have two of them to get."

"OK. See you then." He said.

As we entered the House Chamber, the doorkeeper handed Martin a microphone.

"Mister Speaker, we would ask you to allow us to conduct some very important business in this chamber." Martin said.

"Please enter Agent Butcher and state your business." The Speaker said.

He turned to me and said in a very soft voice; "Hey DJ, you've got the voice, here read this." Martin said and he handed me the file of papers he was carrying and the microphone.

We wrote out what we wanted to say ahead of time so we didn't do any tongue twisters. But I didn't think I was going to read it.

I stood at the door partially hidden behind Martin and his men and read the paper he gave me. One of the few times that I didn't have to talk loud.

"Mister Speaker, the FBI wishes to arrest and take charge of a member of this body based on four criminal charges."

"Who is that member?" He said.

"Congressman Hilliard Rodman Clayton."

"Please read the charges." The Speaker said.

"The charge of first degree murder in the deaths of thirty citizens who were killed at a Country Music concert in Little Rock, Arkansas."

There were some sounds of surprise and disbelief from the people seated there.

"The charge of Terrorism and Terroristic acts against the United States."

More of the same sounds.

"The charge of Espionage against the United States."

Now it has quieted down, but there is still the feeling of disbelief in the room.

"And the charge of Treason against the United States."

Dead silence. I had to take a breath between each charge to be sure I got it right. But I continued.

"The Constitution clearly defines treason as the following. Treason against the United States shall consist only in levying war against the United States, or in adhering to their enemies, giving them aid and comfort."

"No one can be punished for treason until he has been convicted in the courts, or by court martial in time of war. Congress determines by law, what the penalties shall be. Death or life in prison are the usual penalties."

"We will be putting this man on trial for the four listed charges as soon as possible."

I was glad that was over.

"Agent Butcher, you may remove the member from this room." The Speaker said.

Two Agents began to remove the Congressman and he resisted. He suddenly became violent and struggled with them. Another agent grabbed him and he struggled all the more.

This guy Clayton isn't the biggest guy around, even though he must think he is. The three agents weren't doing much to calm him down. The Speaker could see that and he said.

"One Shot would you like to explain all the little details to the Congressman? It looks like he doesn't know our procedures " The Speaker said and I could see him chuckle a little.

I'm glad the Speaker told me ahead of time that he wanted me to do this. This is not where I do my business. Every head turned as I walked by. I took a slow walk down the aisle and stopped directly in front of Clayton. I didn't want him to think I wasn't there for him. Now is one of those times when I'm glad I am wearing a full blown disguise. If any of them saw me tomorrow they wouldn't recognize me.

"So you don't want to go with these men? Let me give you a choice. You can go with them quietly or I can have James Bond speak to you."

I opened my jacket to show him the shoulder holster.

"Mister Speaker, do you know this man? I believe he just threatened me." Clayton said.

"Oh, yes! I am sure he did! I invited him! He is an old friend and he is not encumbered by any of the rules that the others are. You should believe him when he says something. I have seen him work. I am surprised that you haven't heard his name before. One Shot McCoy is well-known all around the country."

There was a little buzz when he said my name.

Clayton looked a little shocked but he made the right decision and picked the FBI. He walked out in handcuffs with them.

"I hope your sentence is not death. I would enjoy visiting you in that little town near Kansas City or even better, in Cuba. They know me in both places."

"I hate you! I will kill you!" He said.

"Yeah! Yeah! Get in line!"

That brought some chuckles from the Speaker and a few friends in the room.

I turned to face the Speaker and said. "Thank you Mister Speaker for the opportunity to finally close this case. I would also like to remind the members here that Clayton and his family are not the only ones who want to destroy us. If there is another with those thoughts in here, he should remember what he just saw. Clayton was the first one of our opponents to walk out alive in a very long time."

Jerry was waiting for me in the hall. We drove immediately to the hotel and I ran to the room to get changed.

Ted was ready to go! After this week,so was I. Ted loves to fly that blue plane and I love to sit back and rest in it. Denise and Vonnie were waiting for us at the airport in Falcon when we landed. Boy was I glad of that.

Boy am I glad that Danbury thing is over, and I finally got a good nights sleep in my own bed. We'll probably be involved a lot more with all those people. I'm sure there will be some that say they were born there. But we'll cross that bridge when we come to it.

I called Lopez, Norm and Earl and said. "It's over! Let's have a big party."

There's always a very positive response when I say that.

Years ago, Mike and I would sit in the back yard in our lawn chairs and drool over everything that the women brought out. Now it's Lopez, Earl, Norm and I in the lawn chairs, but we're all still drooling.

My two girls, Mel and Jen, did all the cooking except for the dishes that the women brought. One of the local PD guys got an elk during hunting season and he gave the girls a box full of elk steaks, and they went over big!

I made some cornhole targets out of old wood. We were throwing the bean bags at the holes on the targets. But we stopped each time that a dish flew out to the tables.

The girls were very busy at the four burner cook-top in the outdoor kitchen all day. But they both love to cook and watch people eat their food.

Everyone was wild about the screenroom. Our party continued all day and into the next. There was no talk about work. Everyone left with a full belly and a smile on their face.

As we were reclining there with our bellies full and a nice cold glass of tea in my hand, Lopez thought of something. I could see it as he sat up and looked at me with that surprised look on his face.

Lopez always knows how to screw up a nice day.

"You do know that you will have to go back there for the trial, don't you?" He said.

Now I need a nap.

Jerry called me to tell me about the arraignment of Clayton.

"I am glad that will be happening, but don't look for me or any of my friends. We don't care about him. Besides, I am sure I will be forced into attending the trial."

"There will be closed circuit television on this one. They are doing it mostly to show others what might happen if they fall onto the same traps as Clayton did." He said.

"You think he fell into a trap? He dug the hole and lined it with money so he could live rich in his home country! I'm rooting for the death penalty, but if they give him a life sentence, I will go to see him just to keep him irritated."

"Do you want me to send you a copy of the tape of the arraignment?" He asked.

"Yes. Definitely! I am sure Ted and Mike and the rest will enjoy it. We'll show it in the conference room at the PD headquarters."

Chapter 19

Some Home Work

We did some preliminary checking on Jane Castle. She lives in Fairfax, Virginia. She belongs to the Christian church, a flower club, a quilt club, she attends all the kids school activities, she attends the PTA meetings, and helps at the food pantry. She is a regular American mom. She has two kids and a dog.

We also found that Jane Castle had prior law enforcement experience from Fairfax before she was married. But this time she was a tourist. She had never been to the WH before and wanted to see it.

She saw this guy acting 'funny' and decided she had better watch him.

I've been married for three decades and I still don't understand the properties that women have where they can see something and know that something is wrong or that someone is acting 'funny'. But I have found that they are always right.

So she began to watch him. In law enforcement we call that surveillance. Since she thought he was acting suspiciously, she decided to help him to find out what he was really doing. That way she could get more information. But why the shoes? He wanted new shoes. I guess he figured she was an available sucker.

Maybe she was. She bought them for him and he wore them out of the store.

The fingerprint on the box had to belong to the guy, since Jane's prints are on file in Fairfax. We still don't know who he is.

After some serious questioning of the guy, we found out why the guy said he tried to steal the TS folder. The guy said he was an aide to a Vermont Representative. He heard about some damaging info on his Rep, and he was going to destroy the information so the Rep wouldn't get in trouble. This Representative could be a terrorist too. We don't know yet. If he is, he's in big trouble. I'm not sure I believe anything that he said.

He took a bus back with Jane following him to Pennsylvania Avenue and he just walked into the White House. Nobody noticed him. She lost him in the crowd until he made his move.

After it was all over I had a chance to talk with her. She belongs to the Tea Party and she offered to help in any way she could. She said that she missed the police work, and that she has friends all over the country. They all say they will call her if they see the bad guys.

"You said that you have already been through the Academy?"

"Yes, but it's been a few years." She said.

"Maybe I could recommend that you have a refresher course and start over."

"I would love that. Besides I would be looking for a better job anyway." She said.

I had to laugh at that.

One thing bothers me. How did he hear about the damaging information, and who told him. There is a serious leak there somewhere. We're still checking on the birth place of this guy.

The preliminary hearing for Clayton was hurried along by the Speaker and his party and many members of the other party also.

I sat in the back out of sight. It didn't take long to hear a few witnesses testify about Clayton and his bunch of terrorists. The unanimous vote to bind him over for trial took only an hour after the attorney for the defense sat down.

No one wanted the embarrassment of this to get out of the building. Everyone was sworn to secrecy. But there's always one bigmouth who thinks he is more important than all the rest. I sure would like to find him!

I found the newspaper that leaked the name and went to see the editor. I talked to the person who took the call and now I have a line on our leak. It was male with an unusual accent. I'm going to hang this one out to dry.

The trial date has been set for about two months from now. Everyone in the Congress and the Media is talking about it. Of course the Media all say the he is innocent, and they just know it because he is such a sweet man. They have a wake-up call coming.

They were walking him down the hall the other day as they were taking him somewhere and as he went past me I said "One Shot" just loud enough for him to hear, but no one else. He jumped like he was stung and looked around but he didn't recognize me in my disguise. This is going to be fun!

But it's time to go! These trips back and forth to DC wear me out.

It's good to get home and get back to the old grind. Kissing my wife and children. Shaking hands with the people in the office and at church. Talking to the business owners and workers that I know. Looking up high in the west and seeing those beautiful mountains. One in particular named after Zebulon Pike.

And I always enjoy helping Earl and Norm and Lopez. Jim is with me now everywhere we go.

I'm going to start going to all the tourist places again, with my friends and family, starting with Cripple Creek. It's all full of casinos now. The first time I went there, we had a picnic lunch in the park on the hill on Bennett Street, the main street of Cripple Creek.

Another place I want to see again is Seven Falls. Just up Cheyenne Boulevard past the Broadmoor. That's another couple of places we haven't been to in years.

There is so much I have missed in the past few years. The Cave of the Winds, Manitou, Fort Carson, the Air Force Academy, and all those planes, Fountain, Security and Widefield, the Will Rogers Shrine, the Garden of the Gods, and a ride on the train to the top of Pikes Peak.

I drove the full length of Academy Boulevard the other day just for fun.

But I haven't forgotten about that leaker in DC. I have a first name now, but not the last.

Jane Castle doesn't have a car. I could get her one from the Foundation. I wouldn't want to put an extension of the Foundation in DC. There are too many politicians who would use it for their own convenience. If she works out, we could fly her to KC and she could drive back home.

I think that's a good idea. I'll run it by Norm, Mike and Ted. Ted said that he would fly her to KC and back.

One of Lopez's lady officers found a Professor who found and corrupted a teacher and another professor to give a job to one of his friends or students.

They will pick up the professor as soon as they locate him. The teacher was innocent, she was only trying to help another teacher. The professor is the guilty one, and we will put him away.

Lopez assigned Jim and I to central downtown. Now we have Weber to the railroad and I-25 to Fillmore. I haven't counted, but that's a lot of blocks to walk or whatever we will do at the time. But, we get all the good stuff, we get to stop in at the office every day and have coffee with the division, then out on the street and have coffee and doughnuts with all of the nice places. We are in the heart of the city.

I'm not complaining, I'm home!

Every day that I come to work early, I get a laugh. Xavier Onassis is on the night cleaning crew, and he locks up just after the sun comes up. I make a point to say 'Hi' to him, but I always laugh a little.

The tapes from Jerry came today. Lopez had some of the officers set up a TV and tape player for the demonstration. This should be good!

Lopez hit the start button and we all sat there quietly.

A male voice began with the following words.

"The following proceedings are presented before the Honorable Keith Baylor, Judge of the Federal Court within Pulaski County, Arkansas."

Two men stood up. "United States Attorney, Nathan Crow, for the prosecution, Your Honor."

"Willard Shaw, Deputy Attorney General of Arkansas for the Prosecution, Your Honor."

Then another man stood up. "James Morris for the Defense, Your Honor.

"Jim, this is going to be a long trial since there are four charges. Have you explained the charges to your client?

"Yes, Your Honor. We have spent many hours discussing this.

"Tom, will you read the information.

The camera went to a man sitting at a small table with files and papers and a computer. He stood and read from one of the pages.

"Charge one. State of Arkansas against Hilliarm Rodman Clayton. That defendant, on or about the 16th day of August of this year, did willfully and feloniously shoot and kill Lillian Ann Waller."

"Charge two. Terrorism and Terroristic acts against the United States."

"Charge three. Espionage against the United States."

"Charge four. Treason against the United States."

The clerk sat down.

"Mister Crow, are you and Mister Shaw ready to go to trial on all charges?"

"Yes, Your Honor. But we have not subpoenaed any witnesses as yet since we did not have a date. But all witnesses have been notified and will be available. We might need a month, though."

"I will give you two."

"Mister Morris, are you ready to go to trial?"

"Yes sir."

"The Defendant is formally arraigned. How do you plead Mr. Clayton?"

"Not Guilty." He said.

"And pleads not guilty."

"Cause set for the nineteenth of October. Is that acceptable to both sides?" The judge asked.

"Yes, Your Honor. Yes, Your Honor. Yes, Your Honor."

"Tom, call the next case."

Lopez turned the lights back on and most everyone went back to their stations.

"Well, he has been arraigned. Maybe he finally believes that we aren't playing games and he is not getting away with this because he is a Congressman. I know I will be subpoenaed for the trial. Do they recess over weekends? I'd like to go home on the weekend and shake it all off."

"I'll probably have to go too. Maybe we can travel together." Lopez said.

After I talked with Ted and Mike about getting a car ready for Jane, I knew I had better run it by Norm. I always love walking around Norm's shop anyway. I sneaked in one night and tried to find something that Norm has hidden among all the ones that really need work. But no matter how quiet and sneaky I am, he always catches me.

I explained my idea about Jane and how she needed a car. Norm said he had a very nice car that I could give to Jane Castle.

I was shocked, but listened intently.

"Mike and Ted agreed, and Ted said he will fly to Fairfax and bring her back here to get the car."

"Come over here and and see it" Norm said. "It's a 1967 Olds Cutlass. It's gold with a black top."

As usual, I was surprised by Norm. He must be psychic or able to see into the future.

It's been a long time since I had a bike ride with my daughters and Harry. It's time.

Denise and I have a little trailer for small things like bikes. We loaded all of our bikes into it and hooked it to the back of my famous '40 Ford VW Woody Wagon and drove to the Garden of the Gods for the day.

We rode all around the park and even stopped at the gift shop for a while. Then we rode down the hill to Colorado Avenue and had lunch. We had a regular parade of bikes. What great fun!

Chapter 20

Big News.

Jerry called me at home the next day.

"What are you going to do about that guy we got here?" He asked.

"Nothing! We don't know who he is. We did prints on him and didn't find anything. Besides, you have all the resources. I'm staying here for a long time, and I'm not planning any trips out of this town for a very long time."

"We did a DNA test, but that didn't tell us very much. He was average." He said. "He was the one in the White House that tried to steal that TS folder."

"Yes, I remember."

"He said that he was trying to clear his boss, the Congressman. I don't believe that either." Jerry said. "We know that a woman helped him with the shoes and he is in jail now. Do you know who she is yet? We don't."

"Yes, we know who she is. Her name is Jane Castle."

"She could be a secretary, girl friend, wife, another terrorist, or just a passer-by." He said.

"You're doing excellent work, Jerry. You'll be a good investigator soon. What if the woman was not a terrorist. Maybe she was just helping a homeless man with shoes and transportation to the shoe store."

"But how and why did he get himself and her into the White House?" He said.

"I can tell you that the woman is not a terrorist. We have checked her out. Now comes your investigation skills. I think you should pass this one off to other officers."

"OK, you're right." He said.

I decided to write out everything about Clayton that I had, and send it to the Director. This will take some concentrating and time.

The information that I have says that Clayton and his whole crew all came from one family in Lebanon. Clayton actually bribed Gerald Madison to make fake birth certificates and file them in the Danbury Courthouse. They show the right ages and vital statistics. All it takes is money!

Mr. Madison said he will will testify for us.

The whole family was taught to say they were born in Danbury except his secretary. That's what they do.

I put down all the facts that I could dig up about this guy. I hoped it would help convict him.

I started with the counterfeiting. I think that Emerson was in the counterfeiting business before Clayton came here. Clayton saw it as another way to undermine the American economy. He became Emerson's partner and when he was elected to be a Congressman, they made the big time.

We have good clear photos of the printing press and all the stuff in the basement.

They had to have help with the printing press in the basement and all the paper, ink and time that is required. They couldn't have done it themselves. So the question is this. Who are we looking for and how many are they?

They brought the whole family and their anti-American terrorist friends. They must have brought many people in many plane loads to Danbury. Even more than their own family. But none of them are working on the money.

Clayton and Emerson got most of them jobs in the Government or in some way connected to the Federal government and other state governments. They were scattered around in different agencies but they all worked together.

We found two guys who saw a truck bring in a fork-lift to the airport office. The fork was used to load a second truck with what looked to them like rolls of paper. There were also two large square wooden crates. When they were done, both drivers took the trucks and their loads away. The huge crates and a printing press were on the one truck and the fork on the other.

It only took them less than an hour to complete the job. They loaded everything out the back door on the dock. It's always locked, so someone had a key. Both guys got a good photo of the drivers and one guy standing in the background. It's Clayton.

The two drivers could be clean. It's hard to tell. But we'll pick them up and quiz them for whatever we can get. After our questioning, both men have said that they will testify for us.

I finally decided to go to the office this morning and confer with Lopez and Jim. There seems to be a lull in the normal crime wave we usually experience every day around here. But as always, there's always a way to screw up a nice day. Here it comes.

A Process Server just walked into our office with a subpoena for me to the trial. I'm to be a witness for the prosecution. I like it. I really want to see this guy put away.

I really expected this but not this soon. There isn't a date on the paper. I'm sure they will call me again for an actual date when it gets closer.

We have lots of evidence on the counterfeiting business they had, but I want more about the terrorism and murder. I took Jim and we went to Danbury for a few days and asked around. We only found two people who remembered anything. But it was sketchy.

We believe that Clayton was born outside the US. We found a funeral director that will testify that a man found out about a dead infant and went to him and paid him to cremate the body with a man and put all the ashes together in the urn he would give to the man's wife. Then he paid the funeral director a large fee for the infant's Social Security number.

We have talked to a man who works in the funeral home where this took place who has agreed to testify to the facts surrounding these happenings.

We have arrested the funeral director and the owner of the funeral home in connection to these events. They have been doing this thing for a long time. I suspect that this is the way that all of the Claytons got their Social Security numbers.

Then we found out that no one had ever run background checks on Clayton, Emerson or any member of the family that they brought over from Lebanon. It seems that someone in the Party was in charge of handling the background checks and they swept it under the rug.

It looks to me like there is something to hide here. And that the person trying to hide it is a very high ranking official. But I don't know who it is right now. Give me a little time. We'll find them.

This whole thing with Clayton and the rest of them is a lot bigger than we ever thought.

We must have terrorists or sympathizers in the House and Senate. This has become a huge problem.

"Hello. This is the Director's office. May I help you?" She said.

"Good morning. This is DJ. May I speak with the Director?"

"Certainly DJ. Please hold on." She said.

"Good morning DJ. You did a wonderful job here in DC. What can I do for you today?" He said.

I explained what we have uncovered and we discussed the ramifications of it and what we should do now.

"I think we should contact Martin Butcher and the Speaker and a few others to get this cleaned up. It looks like we have only seen the tip of the problem." He said.

"You know that all of my friends and I do not want to come to DC and spend forever hunting terrorists disguised as Congressmen, Senators, and maybe even FBI and DOJ personnel. All of us would be glad to hand it over to trustworthy FBI folks."

"From what you have told me that you have found, I don't know who I can trust and who I can't, except you." He said.

"If you insist that we have a meeting, can we do it somewhere outside of DC where we won't stick out so visibly?"

"Certainly! Where would you suggest?" He said.

"Mike's grandfather bought a little bar and grille in Platte City, Missouri many years ago. No one would even notice us there if we didn't all come in at once. And of course, no tuxedos or fancy clothes and no lawyers or reporters. And especially, checks on every one who even knows about this meeting!"

"Perfect! Will you set it up and call me when your team is ready?" He said.

"I'll get right on it!"

I called Mike and asked him to put everything together in KC. I called Lopez and Jim, and of course my darling wife. All three said they would be glad to help.

Ted wanted to fly out and pick us up, but there were too many of us. I rented a bus and conned Earl into being the driver. It will be a vacation for him and I will pay for everything. We all met at Norm's shop and left the cars there.

We had a leisurely trip across Kansas in an air conditioned bus with all our local PD friends.

When I walked into Mike's bar, it was empty and there was a big sign on the front saying "Closed for Remodeling" on the front over the door.

I called the Director's office to notify them that we were ready.

"Everything is set up here in KC sir. We have accommodations for as many as twenty folks if you want. The way I see it, this is going to be a Top Secret operation, no lawyers, no press people. Ted will pick you up at the Sharon Springs airport tomorrow."

"We will be there tomorrow." The Director said.

Earl and I went to KCI to pick up the Director and his associates in the bus and bring them back to Platte City. Earl looks like he is having more fun than all the rest of us.

Sally came over and I introduced her to everyone.

"What do you think?" She said.

"I love it. I can't ever remember seeing this place without someone sitting here."

"We have plenty of rooms here and the hotels close around the block are all empty for you as well. Mike made the reservations. You and Earl will be upstairs in one of the rooms. The others can go pick up their key and pay when they want."

"We have the whole crew coming in tomorrow. Cooks and maids and all the staff in the hotels. Each person will have to take care of their own needs." She said.

There were several meetings during the next few hours and the Director explained what he could do. Martin was next. He told what his FBI guys could do. Then Brown and Lopez said their part. Mike and I and our bunch were left with the legwork. I might have known.

Mike's bar looked like a catch-all from a furniture store. We had tables for desks and phones everywhere. Everyone was eating on the run or at their table/desk.

Brown finally got a break when a background check on a Midwest Congressman turned up with duplicate numbers with someone else.

"Look at this! I have a Congressman in Virginia with the Social the same as a guy in Kentucky with a different name, but the same Social." He said.

Everyone in the room stopped and went to look.

"This might be the break we need!" Martin said. "The Speaker said he would help. I'll call him."

"Mister Speaker, we may have a suspect. Would you please check this guy out for me. I'm sending you his info and a guy in Kentucky as well. You'll see what the problem is." - - - "Yes that's the one. Thanks."

"He said he would get back to me as soon as he had what we needed." Martin said.

Everyone muddled along for another hour until Martin's phone rang.

"This is Martin." He said. "Yes, I have it, thanks."

"We may have found one. Which one of you guys has Virginia in your pocket?" Martin asked.

One of his guys responded and took the info to his table and got on the phone.

"There are five hundred people in Congress and it takes some time to check every one." Martin said.

DNA on Clayton says he came from one of the middle eastern countries but it's so vague.

All military members and veterans have their prints recorded upon entry into the service. It's easy to go through this group for a comparison of the prints.

Martin stood up and walked to the center of the room and began his briefing.

"We don't have much time left before the trial. I would like for each of you to follow up and finish what you have been working on by the first of the month so we can present it all to the Prosecutor. We know what he did, we were there when it happened. Let's make sure that the jury hears every little bit of it." He said.

Mike called the godfather in Pittsburgh as One Shot and asked about a forger who does Social Security cards.

"Sure. His name is Milo and I'll have Jeff get you his address and phone. You tell him that you talked to me. He will tell you anything he knows."

"Jeff and I talked for a minute and he gave me Milo's phone number and I excused myself and called him immediately." Mike said.

"Just before I got off the phone, Jeff said to me, "Aren't you going to ask me about what Clayton did before he was Clayton?"

"Sorry, did I miss something." Mike said.

"It turns out that he was not from Lebanon. He was Secret Police in the Ukraine, where the whole family lived. That's in Russia." Jeff said.

"That was the biggest shock of the month for me." Mike said.

"Milo gave me a whole list of names who were customers. There were Journalists, Politicians, ordinary working guys who were hiding from their families and ex-wives."

"The name Clayton came up several times. He must have sold dozens of Claytons and of course one Emerson."

"I immediately turned over all the names that Milo gave me to Martin and his team. They read them and about jumped out of their skins. There were names of every kind spread around the DC area and some state capitals." Mike said.

"I think I need a break after those shocks." Mike said and went into the kitchen.

Martin called his supervisor in DC and relayed all the information that Mike gave him and there was a long pause while Martin waited for the other end to talk again.

Finally they were back on the line to him. He said that they would take care of the problems in DC. They will try to fill up all the jail cells that they can.

It took a couple days to get all the information ready for the US Attorney, but Martin and his guys delivered it. We searched out customers of Milo and found some, questioned them and had to bring in a few to interrogate them properly. A few of them didn't want to cooperate, but I finally convinced them.

The FBI hunted down several politicians and arrested them. The ones I most enjoyed were the Journalists. They think that they own the world and we all work for them. The ones behind bars are especially loud and offensive.

The one that surprised me the most, was a school teacher or principal or something. He told everyone who would listen, that the words,"In God We Trust" were offensive to him. I made a point to tell him that I would pay his way to any country in the world if he would leave that day. I also showed him the way to the door. He may be in line for some bad feelings.

We did find connections back to Clayton and his family to nearly all the criminals we captured.

Chapter 21

The Trial

Well, it looks like I'm not going to get out of it. That trial is next week, and Lopez and I have an invitation. I have already heard from Mike and Ted and their guys. They are all going too. Maybe we'll have a party at the end of the week.

"Week, hell! You know this is going to drag on as long as the Defense Attorney can do it." Lopez said.

The lawyer who files the suit, chooses the venue, and since it all happened in Little Rock, what better place? The Federal Courthouse in Little Rock, Arkansas.

You can't take a lot of clothes when you fly in one of the smaller planes like the one we have. The Bonanza is pretty big, but there's a limit. There's seven of us. Ted might have to make two trips.

I decided that since I'll need disguises during this thing, I'm going to try to look like a local farmer who came there for the entertainment of it. I took old clothes and dressed like a farmer. I sat on the aisle three rows back from the Prosecutor so I could see everyone.

Ted and Ron are outside the courtroom in case of trouble, and we all have our ear buds in and working.

"Testing, testing. Can everyone hear with these little guys?"

"Well hello cousin. I'm behind the Defense table in the back row." Mike said.

Ted and the rest of the guys responded and we are all listening in on the proceedings with great interest.

I wanted to make it a point to sit through the jury selection. I wanted to see the people's reaction to the questions that the lawyers asked. It was quite a learning experience.

It looked like it would take a month to select the jury. The Prosecutor would question and accept someone, and the Defense Attorney would reject him or her. Then soon the reverse would happen. By the end of three days they had four people seated. By the end of the week, there were six.

Lopez and I would periodically go out for coffee, Pepsi, chicken, ribs, and our phones. Mike, Ted, Jim, Jake and Ron stayed away most of the time, but they did come after us at dinner each day.

It crept along slowly but it finally was completed. All of us got to visit most of the downtown area and the best food in the whole town.

Once the jury was selected, I knew the trial would be starting right away. We all had picked our seats so we could see everyone in the gallery. I picked a seat so I could see the Prosecutor and the Judge and the Bailiffs. I was told it would start at ten in the morning.

"All Rise!" the Bailiff bellowed. "All persons having business before this Honorable Judge of the United States District Court will draw near and be heard! The District Court for the City of Little Rock, County of Pulaski, State of Arkansas is now in session! The Honorable Judge Keith Baylor presiding!"

The Judge entered from the rear door and took his seat, knocked once with the gavel and everyone sat.

Just then, a man two rows in back of me stood up and walked up to the gate. Then he pulled out a 45 and pointed it toward the Judge. I jumped up and punched him in the right ear and he lost his grip on the pistol. I grabbed it by the barrel and hit him in the right kidney with the gun butt. He fell face down on the floor. I put my foot in the middle of his back just in case he might want to change his position.

Here's where these ear buds come in handy for us.

"Courtroom, stretcher!"

In only two minutes, Ted and Ron had run in wearing white jump suits with the red cross on them carrying a stretcher. I showed the guy's gun to Ted and planted it hard in the man's crotch.

"OW!"

They took him away and I sat down as if nothing has happened.

I recognized this guy and whispered quietly into the ear bud. "He's the one who tried to steal the TS folder from Jerry."

I said it as I was looking at him.

"Oops! I think the Judge heard me."

Just then the Judge pointed at me, and spoke loudly.

"You! Approach!"

I walked directly toward him and tried to look innocent of anything.

Then in a low voice with his hand covering the microphone, he said. "Who are you?"

I showed him my badge with three fingers over the front of it. Slowly I moved my fingers aside so he could see the words. Then quickly put it back in the folder and my pocket. The Judge saw it, read it and smiled a tiny little grin.

"I'm surprised." He said.

"We're here to help sir." I said with a smile and took my seat.

The Judge recognized each lawyer for the Prosecution and the Defense and the trial began.

"US Attorney, Nathan Crow, for the Prosecution, Your Honor."

"Arkansas Deputy Attorney General, Willard Shaw, for the Prosecution, Your Honor."

"James Morris representing the Defense, Your Honor."

There were also several assistants for both sides sitting around close to the lawyers tables.

The Judge called on each side to give their opening statements. I had no idea how long something like that would take. Those guys can really talk. Nathan went on about each charge in detail and said that he could and would prove that Clayton had master-minded each little phase of their nefarious operation.

Each of the lawyers can talk. A lot. For a long time. Once the Prosecution was seated, the Defense began and it was the same thing, but in reverse. Clayton didn't do nothin'. He's a great guy and a Congressman and you should revere him.

I really hope that Jim Morris doesn't believe what I heard him just say.

"Gentlemen, it's time for lunch. We will recess till two o'clock, and knocked once with the gavel. Then the Judge said, "Attorneys and you in my chambers." He pointed at me again.

We all followed the bailiff and the judge into his chambers.

"Now! Who are you? Really!" He was talking louder this time.

"This could be classified. Are these guys cleared? Will they tell anyone?"

"You all must keep secrets, and this is one of them." The Judge said to them and pointed his finger.

"I'm known as One Shot McCoy."

"I thought he was a criminal. Did you attorneys know this?"

Only the US Attorney indicated a yes vote, the others just shook their heads. "The Speaker advised me that you and your people would be here for protection." Nathan said.

"You would be surprised how many criminals believe that also. I have been inside places that I never thought possible all over the country. It makes a good cover."

"Does Martin know?"

"Yes. He and I have been friends and worked together for several years now. If you want more verification, the Speaker and the Press secretary know me also."

"You get around."

"I guess we're just special." I said in my best cartoon voice and gave him one of those phony grins and he laughed.

First thing after lunch, the Prosecution began their case. I should've brought my recorder, but I forgot it. I would've liked to hear what these guys said again since I am busy watching the gallery and the doors in case we have any more interruptions.

"My first witness will be Mr. Charles Shelley." Nathan said.

"Call Mr. Charles Shelley to the stand."

"Do you swear to tell the truth, the whole truth, and nothing but the truth?" The clerk said.

"I do." He said.

"Be seated."

"Now then, Mr. Shelley, you are the owner of Danbury Funeral Home, Is that right?" Nathan said.

"No sir. I just work there. I do the embalming."

"You're not the owner?"

"No, sir."

"Can you tell me anything about the business that the funeral home does?" Nathan asked.

"You must mean about what Mr. Clayton wanted us to do for him. A long time ago, a man came to talk to the owner. He wanted us to find a dead infant and cremate the body with an adult man so the ashes would all be together. He paid the owner a large amount and we did it. The ashes were all put into an urn and given to the wife."

"I thought it must have been a relative who couldn't afford the process and that he was doing them a favor."

"But then he wanted the Social Security number of the infant. The owner later received another large payment. A couple of years later Mr. Clayton came in and paid the owner another large amount to do it all again. I decided I had better watch what was going on here." Shelley said.

"Did you recognize or ever see any of these people again?"

"Once in a while. Lots of people would come and go sometimes, but I never got to hear what they talked about. They always went outside or into the owner's office."

"Did you receive any of this money?"

"Yes. I never knew what the extra money was for until the owner was arrested. That's when I found out. He always told me that it was a bonus for Christmas or some other holiday. I worked a lot of extra hours and we really needed the money."

"We know that Clayton was born outside the US. And that Danbury, Connecticut, is where he and his family entered the US." Nathan said.

"We have arrested, Glenn Chester, the funeral director and the owner of the funeral home in connection with these events. They have been doing this thing for a long time."

"There was another time that you heard something unusual, wasn't there?" Nathan said.

"Yes sir. It was after the infant I told you about. Mr. Tarlov, the owner, found a homeless man sleeping in the street. He got him to come to the mortuary for some food. He had some clean clothes for him and he took away the old dirty clothes that he was wearing. They both went into the kitchen and I didn't see the homeless man again."

"I learned to use the computer at night classes and I finally found the homeless guy. The paper said that he just disappeared."

"It was a long time before I actually saw what they did with those homeless people. The boss would get their papers and check them out on the computer and if they didn't have any family, and they were not a vet, him and Clayton would kill them and send the Social Security number to a Post Office box. I got the number right here like you said." Shelly said.

He handed a piece of paper to Nathan.

Nathan handed it to the Judge and said, "Prosecution exhibit one, Your Honor."

"Then later, another guy would come with a big package in a brown envelope for the boss. I always got a bonus on the next holiday. But I got a bonus on almost every holiday."

"Your witness."

"You said that you were paid bonuses after each time that 'something unusual' happened. Is that correct?" Jim Morris asked.

"Not each time. I found a bonus in my paycheck at most of the holidays. I was told it was because I was doing a good job." Shelley said.

"Doesn't that make you complicit with the crooked owner?"

"I don't know.   I don't know what complicit means."

"Being a partner in the scheme."

"No! I never had anything to do with their business! I only do the embalming. The owner does the cremating! I'm just telling you what I saw!" Shelley said.

"That will be all."

"You may step down." The Judge said.

Mr. Shelley looked relieved that the questioning was finished. I could see him heave a sigh of relief.

"Next we would like to call Mr. Glenn Chester.

"You are the owner of Danbury Funeral Home. Is that right?"

"No sir. I am the Funeral Director."

"Can you tell us anything about these homeless men we have just heard about?"

"Well, Clayton seemed obsessive about the Social Security numbers and he would press me to get more of them, but he paid us such huge amounts of money. He told me that I was helping out the people who lived in town, because these guys were sucking away funds that would be going to their kids and their families."

"I didn't know what he was doing with the numbers. I knew that Mr. Emerson had a printing press in the basement at the airport, and that Clayton would go visit him every time he came to our place. I thought that he was sending large boxes out of the country."

"I thought it was only fair to give some of the money to Mr. Shelley, since he was working for us and he worked a lot of extra hours doing jobs for Clayton. He has a wife and family and he needed the money and he never asked where it came from." Chester said.

"Next we would like to call Mr. Nickolai Tarlov."

"You are the owner of Danbury Funeral Home. Is that right?"

"Yes sir. I am the owner."

"Can you tell us anything about these homeless men we have just heard about?"

"Well, Clayton seemed obsessive about the Social Security numbers and he would press me to get more of them. But he paid me such huge amounts of money that I got greedy. He told me that I was helping out the people who lived in town. Because these guys were sucking away funds that would be going to kids and their mothers."

"I didn't know what he was doing with the numbers. I know that Mr. Emerson had a printing press in the basement at the airport. Clayton would go visit him every time he came to my place. I know that he was sending large boxes of money out of the country."

"I thought it was only fair to give some of the money to Mr. Shelley, since he was working for me and he worked long hours doing crazy jobs for me and for Clayton. He has a wife and family and he needed the money and he never asked where it came from."

"You are excused. Next witness."

It sounded to me that these last two speeches were rehearsed and practiced. Both of them blamed Clayton for everything, but they are going to jail anyway.

There were lots of witnesses. I didn't count them or take their names, but all of them had something to say and some had photos of the two aides, Emerson and Clayton. They positively identified the shooters in the photos. Each of the witnesses told their story and the lawyers connected Clayton to each of the shooters.

I was next to be called by Nathan.

When I testified, I told as much of the bad stuff as I could think of. I had written it for weeks. There was a lot. The Prosecution would smile a tiny little one when something really bad would come up.

"Did you see him at the concert?" He asked.

"No. I was too busy killing the terrorists he brought with him."

"Objection!"

"Sustained."

"Did you see any of his people?"

"Oh, yes!"

"When was that?" He asked.

"When I was on the stage looking for him and Emerson when the big light came on. Emerson tried to shoot me, but I was a little quicker."

I thought I would leave out the fact that I shot his two aides.

Mike has been standing against the back wall on the other side of the room for half an hour. I wonder what's going on.

All of a sudden the door flew open against the back wall and two guys with guns rushed in and yelled, "Hands up or we'll shoot!" Then I heard James Bond speak twice.

"Physstt!" Physstt!"

The two guys were lying on the floor and Mike and the rest of my guys were dragging them out into the hall.

The bailiffs came with guns and asked for Mike's gun, which he willingly produced to them.

The Judge was noticeably upset. This was the second time someone has been in his courtroom threatening him and his people.

"Fifteen minute recess! Lawyers and you and your people in my chambers. Now!" He said and he pointed at me again.

"Here we go again, guys."

I could tell he was upset. He was gritting his teeth. He looked me straight in the eye and tried to calm down.

"Did you really have to shoot both of them?" The Judge asked.

"We've done this before, Your Honor. If I had captured one of them, the other one would have shot you." Mike said. "We are against having any of our Judges shot, so we take appropriate action as quickly as we can." Mike said with a slight grin.

"There are obviously more than one of you. How many?", the Judge asked me.

"Six. This is my partner and cousin, Jim McCoy. I pointed to Jim. Cousin Mike McCoy and Jake. Then Ted and Ron. They're not McCoys.", I said.

"How would I get hold of you if I wanted to?"

"Jim and I work in Colorado Springs PD, Mike and Jake are in Platte City, and Ted and Ron are part-time In Kansas City."

"We take turns on duty days and weeks. Today was Mike's duty. Good thing! The crooks don't know who we are, where we're from, or where we live. Actually no one knows outside of our team, a few in DC and now you all."

"It appears that you can change your appearance."

"Yes, I have many disguises, like this one now."

"You are wearing a disguise now?"

"I never appear in public without one. It's too dangerous for my family. But I look a little like my cousins."

"I see. Now about these Claytons you keep talking about!"

"There were eighteen in this chain migration. We got seventeen so far, that only leaves one to go."

Martin was there in the back and he said. "That one we got the first day was number eighteen."

"Does this sort of thing just follow you around or are you able to see into the future when someone is going to shoot someone?"

"We all had several meetings before the trial. The FBI agreed with us that there would be someone trying to get Clayton off. We expected trouble, none of us knew what it might be. Every one of us will shoot someone who is threatening the life of a citizen without cause."

"You're the only one with an SS badge, is that right?" The Judge asked.

"Yes, Your Honor."

"Nathan, Jim, let's hurry this along. It looks like we could have more unwanted visitors."

On the fourth day after the Judge had recessed for the day, Lopez and I were walking to another restaurant close to the courthouse when this guy approached us.

He asked, "Who are you guys and what are you doing out here?'

I reached my right hand into my jacket and said, "I'm One Shot McCoy and who wants to know?"

"I don't believe you. I know One Shot and he doesn't look anything like you. And he carries."

"Really? You mean like this?" I used my left hand to open the jacket and with the right hand I showed him James Bond up close and personal.

"I don't know you! What about you? Are you carrying?"

Just then two men in suits with pistols ran up to us and said, "You're under arrest!"

Lopez began to laugh and I am smiling a big one.

All three of them show badges and bring out handcuffs.

I still have my ear bud in, so I said, "Are you listening to this? It's time to show yourself."

Mike and the guys came running out to us. All of them are showing their pistols and laughing.

"What's so funny?" The first guy asked.

"You really don't know, do you? Get those handcuffs!" Mike tells them that I am his prisoner. He took the handcuffs and asked for their badges and cards.

"Who do you work for?" Mike asked.

"We are FBI." He said.

Ted is already on the phone. "Hey Martin, where are you?"

"Still in the court. What's up?"

"We're all outside in the street. Could you look out here and tell me if these guys belong to you?"

Martin came running out into the street and looked at the three guys.

"Well! Well! Well! Yes I do know them. For some reason they always seem to be on the wrong side of things. Ted, you can put those handcuffs on each one of them, and bring them inside where we have a nice little cell just for them for the night."

"This one is Carlos Novak and he is known for funny money. One Shot, maybe you should talk to him about Clayton. That is why you're here isn't it, Carlos?" Martin said.

"What? I don't know anybody named Clayton." He said.

"Oh, this is going to be fun! Lopez and I are going our for dinner now. Guess who will be dinner if we don't get some answers."

"Now this one, Steven Hunter, is supposedly the smart one. He is probably involved in the Concert we all know about here in Little Rock." Martin said.

Mike popped up and said in a loud excited voice. "I'll take him and the rest of the guys can help me question him. I hope he gives me the wrong answers, then we will only have two of them to fool with."

That brought a smile on Mike's face and the rest of them except for the concert guy.

"And I will take this one, I won't tell you his name just yet. He always makes me laugh. Before I put him in jail." Martin said.

We all had dinner and then we took our prisoner to a room and I did my favorite thing. Interrogation! Carlos Novak was a little obstinate, but after having a close relationship with James Bond and understanding what he could do, Carlos began to tell me all about the printing press and the counterfeiting operation. He even told me where the money was sent and the names of the recipients. That is what a little polite questioning will produce.

When we returned from the break, the Judge advised the two counsels that we should move on to the other charges.

When the discussion about counterfeiting came up in court, Nathan called Carlos to the stand. Carlos spilled his guts there and another nail was driven into Clayton's coffin. I was smiling the whole time, since I had loosened Carlos' tongue for him. His leg will be sore for a while and the limp will go away after a few months.

"The money that we made was used for the re-election of Clayton and all of his friends." Carlos said.

"Did you hear that Mike? Clayton was raising money for elections of more terrorists. We need to find out who they are and get rid of them too."

All during the trial Clayton sat there with a big smile and acted like it was all for TV and he would not be convicted of anything or even be thought of as a little bad. But he was wrong.

It took an hour and a half to get through charge number two, but we finally moved on.

I had told Martin about Nema and he had interviewed her several times and had written and audio records of what she had to say.

Nema Jabbar gave a big list of names of terrorists who were working with Clayton's family and his closest workers. She had a complete list of these people when her mother was killed. She gave the list to me months ago and I gave it to Martin and Nathan.

All of the names were completely checked out and found to be terrorists working in Europe, Asia ans America. All with the common goal of destroying all governments which are run by people who are or believed to be Christian. I hope all of them are being rounded up and put in a corral for life.

"Why do you have this list of names?" Nathan asked.

"My mother was a patriot in Egypt and she kept a list of the people who were trying to overthrow the government there. An assassin killed her in Kansas City. Mr. McCoy saved me from him." She said.

The last of the four charges was the most serious. Treason is not a word that you want anyone to even think about you, let alone say it out loud.

Everything that has been presented has been tied to Treason by Nathan and Willard Shaw. They have made each piece of the puzzle fit together into a cohesive picture.

As a final huge spike in Clayton's coffin, they called an unknown man from the gallery.

"Call Andrew Sameer."

"Andrew Sameer to the stand."

"Mr. Sameer, you have said that you have known of and had been associated with Mr. Clayton for a long time. How long?"

"All of my life."

"Please expand on that if you will."

"When we were in school as children, he really hated the American people. Not the ones in the East, because he said they thought like he did. But he hated Christians more. He said that they think they are better than us. He complained that they are always sending our people their little book to read or reading it to them."

"Later, once he was in this country, he preached to Easterners his ideas every day. He told them that they should like gun control. He told them that if there were less guns available to the Americans, they would have less crime. And most of them believed him."

"He said that they should not like the free speech thing because he would have to listen to their lies. And a free press should only print his side of the story, because he was always right."

"The biggest thing was this. He tried to get rid of anyone who disagreed with him or who would show him something on TV that was true. He would make up lies and have them read on the radio as if they were that day's news."

"He told me that he was sure that killing a Christian was not a crime in his country." Sameer said.

"Is that all of it?"

"There is one more thing. He always asked this question. "Why are they following the confused writings of old crazy rebels from hundreds of years ago?"

"He said that the US Constitution should be repealed completely and someone like him should write the truth. And if he has to overthrow the country to do it, he will." He said.

The witness was turned over to the Defense, but Every time Jim Morris asked a question, the answer came back bad for him. He was being overwhelmed by the sheer amount of evil from Clayton and all his friends and relatives.

After Sameer was finished with his testimony, one last witness was called by the prosecution.

"Call Boris Roshenko."

Boris was seated and Willard asked. "What is your job? Why are you here?"

"I am the Ambassador to the United Sates from Russia."

"Do you know anything specific about the defendant?"

"I am glad to hear that the whole family is dead now. They were all scum. But you said there is one more. Do you know who it is? I do. His name is Anatoli Gurdin. He is very bad, maybe the worst of them all. You will find him at the Department of Farming or whatever you call it. He is trying to grow poison corn to feed to the Americans." He said.

"Your witness." Willard said.

Jim's face registered surprise at what he just heard. I am sure he expected a glowing endorsement of Congressman Clayton.

"How do you know this?"

I'm sure Jim is trying to get something good about Clayton to be heard by the jury. So far, it's going from bad to worse.

"They all come from a little town named Sambir in the Ukraine."

"How do you know that Clayton is from Sambir?"

"I too am from Sambir. I have watched him for decades."

Jim finally gave up and sat down.

"The Prosecution rests, Your Honor."

The Judge adjourned the court for the day and the Defense will begin tomorrow.

I can tell that Jim Morris is bewildered about this client he was forced to take on by the government. They couldn't find a lawyer anywhere that would defend this creep. Jim was appointed by the Department of Justice partly because he lived in Arkansas and partly because someone there knew his name.

Jim worked very hard, but it was one step forward and two steps back. He was done and done in.

"Jim said that Clayton demanded to be put on the stand so he could defend himself. I have always heard from lawyers that it is a bad move. We'll see.

When Clayton finally got on the stand and I knew this was his last hurrah. He has been overwhelmed by the Prosecution and their witnesses. Clayton has been crooked and evil for all of his life and now he must pay he piper.

He began talking about his family and his aides. He blamed them for everything. Then there was Emerson who he said was a good guy, but it was his fault he got into counterfeiting. Then he turned on his secretary, who lusted after him. She has been fired and is now in a local jail in DC.

He went on and on about how everybody else was the problem and nothing that was said here was his fault. How could it be his fault? He is Superman and he fixes everything. He should write a book called 'It's not my fault!'. He has no concept of what is around the corner for him. I hope I can be a part of it.

Clayton finally ran out of steam and the Defense rested. It's almost over and Clayton cut his own throat during that last tirade. I feel sorry for Jim Morris after all this.

The judge told the jury all about what they should and shouldn't do and sent them off to deliberate their verdict.

As we walked out, I finally got to see and speak to Clayton. I only said two words, very quietly and very closely to him. "One Shot." He jumped a little and he wasn't very happy about it. I can imagine he is a little worried now. Wait till he sees me, or whoever I'm disguised as, again. I'll make it a point to show him James Bond. See, I'm already laughing about this trial.

It's Friday and now we have to wait over the weekend to finish this fiasco.

Monday morning was the last of it. The Judge came into the court at exactly ten o'clock.

"All rise! All persons having business before this Honorable Judge of the United States District Court will draw near and be heard.! The District Court for the city of Little Rock, County of Pulaski, State of Arkansas is now in session. The Honorable Keith Baylor presiding!"

"Has the jury reached a verdict?"

"Yes, Your Honor."

"Tom, will you receive the verdict from the Foreman?"

The clerk took the paper with the verdict to the Judge who then asked, In the matters at hand how do you find Mr. Foreman?"

The foreman stood and even though he had the words written, he was nervous and shaking as he began to read.

"For the charge of Murder in the first degree, we find the defendant guilty as charged."

I could see him stop and take a breath.

"For the charge of Espionage against the United States, we find the defendant guilty as charged."

It's not getting any easier for him.

"For the charge of Terrorism and Terroristic acts, we find the defendant guilty as charged."

Only one more.

"For the charge of Treason against the United States, we find the defendant guilty as charged."

I could see he was exhausted and was glad that was over when he finally sat down.

I saw this coming and I moved to the seat directly behind Jim Morris.

When we were going out I caught Jim standing in a corner hiding his face from the reporters who were there.

"Jim! Come with me! Quick!"

We ducked into the men's room without being seen.

"Take off your tie and give it to me." He did and I stuck it into my back pocket.

"Now unbutton a couple of buttons on the shirt. Ruffle it up a little. Good! Now put this on."

I dugout a piece of a mask I had in my jacket pocket. I helped him put it on correctly and then I dug out some ladies makeup to hide the seam where the mask fits over the skin. It took some time but now he is his brother.

"It's nice to meet you John Morris. Isn't your brother that famous lawyer Jim Morris?"

He looked into the mirror and said. "Yes, he is." He is now smiling a huge smile, shaking my hand and thanking me.

"Follow me!"

We walked around the swarm of reporters without a single look from them. When we got to our rental car, Lopez began to laugh.

"I see you have been working hard. You look great, DJ, but who is this with you?" He said.

"This is John Morris and we are going to give him a ride to anywhere he wants right now. Let's get out of here."

The next day the Judge talked with the Prosecution and Jim and they decided to do the sentencing today.

"I see no reason that we cannot finish this trial and pass sentence today."

There was a little noise from the reporters in the room. The Judge gave a knock with his gavel and said.

"The court will come to order."

The chatter stopped and the Judge began again.

"Mr. Clayton. You have been found guilty of all charges and I sentence you to life in prison. You will serve that sentence in the Federal Prison located in Leavenworth, Kansas. Court adjourned."

And with one knock with the gavel it was all over.

Chapter 22

Home Again

The trip home was a lot of fun. Earl drove the bus like a pro. We went directly to Platte City and stayed overnight at Mike's place. Lots of food and drink and lots of friendly talk. I could have stayed a few days, but the others had to get back to work and to their homes.

Then seven hundred miles to the Pikes Peak Region. All of our cars were left at Norm's shop, and we all left our car keys with Norm before we left for the trial. So Earl dropped the bus there. We'll get it tomorrow.

All of our cars were left inside the fence or the building and I have keys to get in if we arrive in the middle of the night. When we drove up, there was one car right in front of the door. Norm left us a message. It was an old Dodge Caravan with a new paint job that matched the green van that Earl drives. But there was one very distinct difference. In the driver's side rear window was a stained glass window with the words "Springs Stained Glass" and a phone number cut into it.

We all stood and laughed as we gathered around the car. Maybe Earl will start a new trend.

Norm laughed a lot while he handed out the car keys and told us about any repairs that were made to each of the cars.

I'll be on the phone tomorrow to all our contacts to tell them what the results of the trial were.

But first, the family!

When I finally got home, Denise was very glad to see me. But I could tell that she had something on her mind besides me. We hugged and she looked at me like I should read her mind and say something about whatever it was that she was thinking.

Finally I deduced that she was in a hurry to show me a new addition to our place. She was talking very fast as she dragged me out the back door and across the yard. My mind was still in 'bus rider', so I didn't get any of what she said.

"Come on! Come on!" She is very excited and pushing me out the door.

"You know I always wanted a gazebo, so I called Jason and he and several of his friends came over while you were gone this time and built this on a weekend. I love it!" Denise said. "The girls and I have been out here every day since they finished it."

Denise and I walked around this magical round wooden structure. It is magical for Denise, at least, and it really is a beauty.

Jason really knows his business. Dee and I sat there and talked until the kids finally saw us and they all came out and everyone talked at once for almost an hour. One good thing about coming home after a trip like this is that I get hugs from everyone. Lots of hugs.

A transcript of a mysterious meeting turned up on the floor of a conference room in the Capitol. The papers were given to a secretary in the FBI to record and pass on to Martin.

The papers were recordings of a meeting between two American agents and a foreign agent in the town of Montgomery about his contacts with agents from the US Government.

They were working with some guy from Montgomery. No one gave it any thought until a night staffer found the town named Montgomery in Pakistan near the big city of Lahore.

He spent two weeks tracking this guy and all our suspicions were bearing fruit. What gave it away was the last name of the contact there was Laudin.

The name Montgomery was mentioned in a offhand manner and no one gave it any credence. It gave you the idea that Montgomery was in Mississippi or somewhere in the country. Who would have thought that a town in Pakistan would be named Montgomery?

Some of the dialog of the interrogator and a Pakistani agent(suspect) goes on as follows.

"Who did you meet?" the American asks.

"I dunno. Some Senator and another guy that said he was a Congressman."

The foreign agent said that he was then offered a large suitcase full of money by the two people.

"They said that 'maybe this will help your memory'."

"Do you know their names?"

"No. But I got pix. I always take pix of anyone I meet with."

"Could I see them?"

"Sure."

"Well. Well. Well. Look who's here! Swartz and Felliosi!"

The interrogator now speaks to someone else in the room.

"This is all we need to bring them in. Use handcuffs!"

"Where is the video you said you made?"

"I sent it to the address that they gave me. I have it with me. Here it is. I don't know whose address this is."

"I know this address! We need a Search Warrant for this address! Right away!"

When the rumor of a video of the meeting turned up, the rumor was that Baltazar Ozuma had it. A Search Warrant was issued and the house was searched for the missing video. They found it in the bottom drawer of a four drawer file cabinet under a pile of books and papers.

"Where did you get this video file?" Martin asked.

"I don't know what that is. I have never seen that before." Ozuma said, raising both hands in front of him and shaking his head.

It's hard to do anything but tell the truth on a video recording, but some guys do it. Face to face is much easier. The two of them are on TV for all to see, offering money to a Pakistani agent. They also mentioned names of some of their donors and friends.

The transcript was interesting, but the video was surprising! Whoever did the transcript really worked hard. Most of it was word for word. Some of the words were surprising.

Someone in DC found that the house minority leader was in cahoots with Clayton and his friends. I'll never know how they find out these things, but this guy is in trouble! .

The house minority leader, Felliosi, was taken out and charged. The senate minority leader, Schwartz, was also taken out and charged with something. I didn't find out what it was, for these two to be removed from office, the charges must be big-time serious.

I have worked for the American Government for almost all of my life and I don't understand how some people decide to hate it so fervently.

I don't know a lot, but I do know this. if you're a minority, you want to be a majority, and sometimes people go the wrong way to get where they want to go.

The phone rang and it was Jerry.

"Hey! How are you doing now that the case is wrapped up?" He said.

"Clayton went to Leavenworth. He could have put his hatred in a bag and buried it, but he wanted to show it off to everyone that would say how great he was to have it. Now look what it got him."

"I think I'll go by that little town near Kansas City and visit all my friends who live there. And the guards I know."

"I can't help it, I just have to stop by and say 'Hi' to him. The whole mind-set of Clayton made me laugh. I could go see him. I could say ONE SHOT out loud over the PA system. I could wear a disguise or not. I don't know what I want to do."

"Why would you need a disguise?" Jerry said.

"No disguise? Maybe a little one. He still doesn't know what I look like."

"Forget about him DJ, There's lots more out there waiting for us. And they don't know what you look like either. Ha. Ha." Jerry said.

Jerry really enjoys making those little jokes when I'm around and when I'm the butt of those jokes.

"OK! OK! I give up."

I really do want to know more of the facts about the Little Rock thing.

"What were the results of the Massacre in Little Rock and the following trials and others?"

"Thirty dead, more than that hurt, Clayton in jail, the rest of his family dead. His secretary is in jail, not for long, though. One of the prosecutors was going to give her a break with the charge called 'Misdemeanor Solicitation', but the others wouldn't hear of it. She was charged with 'Conspiracy to Commit a Terrorist Act'. But she was always under orders of Clayton." Jerry said.

"I think she will probably get five years." Jerry said. And if the guy who wanted to go easy on her has his way, she will be out and in his arms in a lot less.

"A new man was appointed to take the Congressman's seat. I sure hope he's not like his predecessor." Jerry said. "Did you know that the Speaker wanted to publicly praise you?"

"Yes, and I flatly refused! I don't want anyone to know that I had anything to do with any part of this case! I will think about retiring if this comes out. When he brought that up to me, I told the Speaker face to face. not to do it. I also added that I won't be there if he does."

"I might help you once in a while if you have a specific job that we could do, but no more of this racing around the country doing footwork when you have at least two other agencies that can do that. I'll be living in my back yard and not leaving town for a very long time."

"As they say in Hollywood. Don't call us, we'll call you!"

I try to go see Norm every day. Mostly just to see what special vehicles he has found and what he has done with them. Since the thing in Little Rock, I have been thinking about what we could do to help.

The Foundation does cars. We don't know how to help a Little Rock victim, but we tried. Norm had several cars and pickups ready to go, so we had a truck deliver a load to the Little Rock Police Station.

I thought they would be better at getting them to the right people. But that's not enough.

"I know a guy that drives a truck and I could get him to take a truckload of something to them." Norm said.

"I've never been in this situation before. I don't know what we could do that would be the best thing for them."

"Why don't we just send money to pay for funerals?" Norm said.

"Good idea! We do have some money. I'll call the Chief there and find out where to send it."

I made a call to Little Rock to get some information. The Chief was very willing to help with my crazy plan.

"How much is a funeral there?"

"I think they could do it for about five grand." He said.

"Would fifty thousand help? I could send it today."

"That would be great, and it would take the pressure off of the families, too. Thanks." He said.

I went to the bank and sent the money right then.

I drove by Earl's place the other day and he had that Dodge Caravan parked near his driveway with the stained glass window showing, What a great billboard! I laugh every time I see it.

The Hare Psychopathy Checklist Items

1. Glibness, Superficial Charm
2. Grandiose Sense of Self-Worth
3. Need for Stimulation
4. Pathological Lying
5. Manipulation
6. Lack of Remorse or Guilt
7. Shallow Effect
8. Lack of Empathy
9. Parasitic Lifestyle
10. Poor Behavioral Control
11. Promiscuous Sexual Behavior
12. Early Behavior Problems
13. Lack of Realistic Goals
14. Impulsive
15. Irresponsibility
16. Failure to Accept Responsibility for own Actions
17. Many Short-term Marital Relationships
18. Juvenile Delinquency
19. Revocation of Conditional Release
20. Criminal Versatility

Wake Up Teachers

The United States of America was founded by a small group of people fleeing from the religious oppression of England in the 1600's.

These people were Christians and they founded a Christian Nation. The Christian name hearkens back to Jesus the Christ. Consequently this country also reaches back to Israel since Jesus was a Jew.

Nowhere in all the words that have been written or spoken over the many years of existence of this country has the word Muslim ever been spoken about the foundation of this country.

The United States is not now, nor ever will be a Muslim nation.

The liberal press and all the misguided principals and teachers in all the schools across this country would do well in reining their ranting about wanting this country to be a Muslim country.

It's long past time for an overhaul in the teaching profession and their unions.

www.ingramcontent.com/pod-product-compliance
Lightning Source LLC
Chambersburg PA
CBHW072234170626
46813CB00003B/1225